love luck

BY SAMANTHA MACKENZIE

The **Magic of the Vampire** Saga

love / *luck*

pure / *evil*

For more titles, visit

SamanthaMacKenzieBooks.com

SAMANTHA MACKENZIE

love luck

MAGIC OF THE VAMPIRE

ONE

This book is a work of fiction. All names, characters, organizations, places, events, and incidents in this book are either products of the author's imagination or used fictitiously. Any resemblance to actual persons, living or dead, or actual events is coincidental.

Cover design by Maria Spada
mariaspada.com

Typeset in 12/16 pt Garamond
Interior design and production management
by Samantha Brennan

This edition edited in US English

A catalogue record for this book is available from
the National Library of Australia

ISBN: 978-0-6450328-0-2 (paperback)
ISBN: 978-0-6450328-1-9 (e-book)

For my husband, who is proof of such a thing
as soul mates at first sight

Dreamer's Log: Margaret
Day Ten of October, Year 1665

Last night I dreamed great change was upon us, and that today I would kill the devil.

I was to dip my fingers into dust made of magic, and then reach into the devil's chest and take purchase of his cold, still heart. I was to drag him down into slumber with me, and by force compel his unnatural soul into the oblivion beyond the aether. I was to obliterate his essence and sever his tether to Earth. I was to rid the world of his evil, forever and ever!

But today, when I arrived at the place where his body had fallen, no sign of him remained.

I still have his magic dust, and in my possession it will remain, for should he reclaim it, the world would be lost again. I have put the dust in a silver pouch and hidden the pouch inside a dream, where no demon can find it. There it will stay until the king of hell himself comes to demand it of me.

I have no doubt he will, for without it, he is nothing.

CHAPTER ONE

My great-grandmother gave me my first pair of silver earrings when I was born. They were finely wrought four-leaf clovers, and I still wore them on my earlobes.

Grams believed that clover was lucky, and she liked to tell people she was Irish, but as far back as anyone can remember, my family has never lived anywhere in Europe. I think we'd need to go back a couple hundred years to find the origins of our "Irish" blood, and I've told Grams that more than once. Most days I tried hard not to say things that might end in an argument—despite our differences, Grams was everything to me and the only family I had—but we were both genetically predisposed to speaking our minds without first considering the consequences.

Grams and I lived in a compact two-bedroom house on the far outskirts of a small town a little way north of Byron Bay, in the east-coast subtropics of Australia. Grams didn't much like the heat, but we'd moved here when I was twelve, right after my mother died, and she insisted it was where she wanted to be. I wasn't in love with the sun myself, thanks to my textbook *Irish* coloring—ivory skin that couldn't tolerate UV and copper hair that would never look sun-bleached—but I didn't want to move either. It wasn't as though I'd grown used to the heat in the last five years. I just kind of liked having a convenient excuse to be moody and miserable.

Today was going to be particularly uncomfortable, I could tell. It was only eight a.m. and already too warm. I stood in the tiny bathroom Grams and I shared, feeling momentarily refreshed after a cool shower. Dressed in my usual denim shorts and a loose-fitting tee, I swiped a slick of sunscreen across my nose and then pulled my long, heavy hair off my neck. I held it there with one hand while I used the other to grope around in the drawers for an elastic band.

"Riley?" Grams's reedy voice was punctuated by the light rap of her swollen knuckles on the other side of the closed bathroom door.

"Come in," I said, my fingers finally catching on a band stuck in the far corner of the bottom drawer. I pulled it out, and then deftly twisted and secured my hair into a loose knot at the top of my head.

The door creaked on its hinges as Grams pushed it open. Neither she nor I knew our way around a toolbox, so things like stiff hinges, broken doorknobs, and flaking wall paint were domestic realities to which we'd become accustomed.

Grams's lined face smiled at my reflection in the vanity mirror. She reached up to stroke the silver clovers on my ears. "The luck of the Irish," she said.

I grabbed her hand and firmly returned it to her side.

Grams's belief in things like lucky earrings irritated me, and while I tolerated her eccentricities, I never actively encouraged them. And yes, I wore the silver clover studs to keep Grams happy, but they weren't the only jewelry decorating my ears—and the other pieces were all for me.

I had the one piercing in my right ear, but six in my left: two extra studs in the lobe, a sleeper in the tragus, a cuff on the auricle, and another stud on the helix. All silver. Most people assumed they were a sartorial act of teenage rebellion, but that really wasn't the case. Grams liked them—encouraged them, even. She herself had six rings in each earlobe and a stud in her nose.

Grams was an odd one. She was incredibly superstitious, obsessed with silver jewelry, and preoccupied with dreams, and, although it was all nonsense, I suspected it was Grams's quirks that had kept her alive this long. She couldn't die if she had to be here to protect me, heathen that I was, from those pesky demonic predators who hunted in the night.

"Did I hear someone at the door?" I asked, changing the subject.

"Finn just arrived."

"Finn's here?"

I snatched up my toothbrush and frantically foamed up my mouth. I usually met my best friend at school on weekday mornings, so his appearance here at this hour on a Monday was unexpected.

Grams's eyes crinkled above a knowing smile, and I ignored her.

"Finn, yes, and Harry, and a few...others," she said. "They're here for an early Monday meeting."

I spat into the sink, cupped my hands to collect the water from the faucet, and rinsed out my mouth to give me a few extra seconds to moderate my response.

I'd hated Mondays since I was twelve, and not for the reasons most people hate them—well, not entirely the same. The first day of the school week was designed to always suck, but my reasons were more complicated than that.

Even as a kid, I knew people thought my Grams was weird. When we moved here, I thought the upside would be we could start over. Act *normal*. I never could have predicted that Grams would find a bunch of people as bent on superstition as she was, but that's just what she did. The moving truck had barely left the driveway by the time Grams had sniffed out the name of someone nearby who believed in all the same weird stuff she loved: silver charms, dream-reading, fortune-telling, and demon-mongering. That person knew others like him, and soon word got around that Old Maggie Quinn had moved to the neighborhood, and she was the person to go to for all things *woo*. Grams had set up a regular Monday meeting soon after that, and now once a week my home became the headquarters for every loon in town.

It was only days later that I started at the local school, where I'd met Finn. We bonded instantly because, to his extreme frustration, that first guy Grams had found was Finn's dad, Harry, and all the others like him were the people in Finn's family.

If anyone despised Mondays as much as I did, it was Finn.

"Right," I said curtly. I threw my hairbrush into a drawer and pecked Grams on the cheek. Sliding around her, I collected my schoolbag from the hallway floor and dashed to the staircase.

Finn waited for me at the bottom, smiling widely as usual. His straight white teeth were bright against his sun-darkened skin, and I let myself admire his face for a brief moment. Everything about him was my opposite. His blonde hair had lightened over the summer, thanks to day after day spent in the surf, his broad shoulders were bronzed, and his eyes were warm and brown. I always felt paler, softer, and moodier standing in the shadow of his golden skin, toned arms, and sunshine smile.

I leaped over the last two steps and landed with a thud beside him, and he wrapped me in a hug that made my ribs creak.

"Back to school, finally!" he said with bogus cheer. "Are we excited?"

He dropped his arms, and I bared my teeth in an equally phony smile. "Sure. Can't you tell?"

"Riley-Rae, we've been friends since seventh grade. I know you better than you know yourself. Your face says, 'kill me now,' but inside, you're all about the happy dance.

Tell me I'm wrong."

He grinned at me because he already knew my answer, and I rolled my eyes. Finn did know me better than anyone else, almost as well as he thought he did. School wasn't my favorite place to be, and there wasn't much about today that I was looking forward to.

"You're wrong," I confirmed, and then I looked up at him with sad eyes and a furrowed brow. "Can't we skip today? I've got a great book weighing down my backpack. We could pick up some food, sneak into somewhere with air-conditioning?"

"And miss the first day back?" Finn shook his head. "Let's save your excellent plan for later in the year, okay?"

I'd expected his answer, so I dropped the pathetic expression and shrugged noncommittally.

Finn cared less about school than I did, barely passed his classes, and only showed enthusiasm when it was time to play sports, but for some reason, he insisted I take my education seriously. He was convinced I was destined for university or something, and despite his own clear lack of study ethic, all the teachers loved him because he was just so *beautiful*—in every sense of the word. Any girl in our school would trip, then step over, their best friend to get their hands on him.

I led the way down our short hallway, planning to zoom past the living room with a vague wave in that direction, but I froze before I reached the front door.

When Grams had said there were others here besides Finn and his father, Harry, I'd assumed she'd meant the extended

O'Brien family—and there were a lot of them. And yes, our small living room was crowded, as I had expected it to be, but something was different today. The buzz of Grams's usually rowdy group was muted—everybody spoke so quietly there was barely a hum of conversation—and there were too many people I didn't recognize. That by itself was unusual enough, because everyone knew everyone else in our small town and the tourists were easy to pick out, but the unfamiliarity of these people wasn't the oddest thing about them.

The strangers were three men and one woman, all dressed in clothes too long and dark to suit our local weather. Their skin was pale—paler than mine, if that was possible—and all had glossy hair in barely varied shades of deep, dark brown. The oldest of the four had gray streaks at his temples.

As I hovered awkwardly in the doorway, every one of those strangers looked up, and four carefully composed, impossibly perfect faces considered me without speaking a word. Each pair of eyes was so dark, they looked almost black.

I stood there, confusion and discomfort rooting me to the spot, until Grams jostled me a little as she shuffled past, and I closed my mouth with an audible click.

I didn't like to use language my great-grandmother would approve of, but even I could sense the energy in the room, and I had the uncomfortable feeling I'd interrupted something.

I took an involuntary step backward and landed on Finn's toes. He'd stepped up close behind me to get his own look at Grams's guests, and now he glared at them over my head, the muscles in his jaw feathering with tension.

"Ah, Riley," Grams said, extending her hand to invite me into the room. I took a slow step forward, and then another, reaching Grams in a few more steps. I took her hand, and she grasped my fingers tightly.

Finn stayed where he was, arms folded across his chest.

"Riley," Grams repeated. "I'd like you to meet some new acquaintances. Perry Callaghan, his sons Leo and Noel, and their friend, Adeline Bennet."

The visitors nodded in turn as Grams called their names. Perry was the oldest of the four—about the same age as Finn's dad, maybe a few years his senior—but still handsome. Leo and Noel must have been at least five years older than me, and both had big shoulders and wide chests. They looked so alike they had to be twins. Adeline, with her masses of wavy hair, long dark lashes, and delicate, impeccably proportioned features, eyed me coolly. She seemed particularly offended by my earrings, her gaze returning more than once to take inventory of my left ear. She wore no jewelry of her own that I could see. Adeline looked a similar age to the younger men, and she sat nearest to Noel. My suspicions about their closeness were confirmed when he reached out and took her hand in a gesture that struck me as an attempt to reassure her.

"Hello," I said lamely, not understanding the vibe in the room. I'd come to expect the quirks in character and unconventional behaviors typical of the people Grams liked to associate with, and I was no longer surprised when

I found her chanting, or translating the meanings of dreams, or handing out the silver jewelry she made with her own arthritic hands, but this…this was different.

"Hello, Riley," Perry replied, nodding politely. His lips were pink and plump, and his white teeth glistened behind them as he spoke. "It's very good to meet you. Your grandmother has told me so much about you."

His words seemed to hiss very slightly, as though he had a lisp or something. It wasn't unpleasant in the least, and I found myself waiting for him to speak again so I could listen for the sound. He watched me with expectation.

"Ah, that's nice," I said finally, disappointed that he hadn't said more. My eyes traveled over his lips and teeth as I tried to work out how he could form such soft, pleasing sounds, and the corners of his mouth curved up in a perceptive smile. My heart sped up, and I flushed slightly in embarrassment.

Finn took a sudden step into the room, and all heads swung in his direction.

Harry's bass voice rumbled around the room. "Perry and his family share our interests in dreams and demons," he said, his eyes locked on his son. "They have new ideas about things—interesting ideas. We might be able to learn something."

Something in Harry's words must have penetrated Finn's mood, because my friend dropped his arms and looked at me. "Come on, Rae," he said, his nonchalance sounding forced. "We're going to be late for school."

I gave Grams's hand one last squeeze, avoided looking at anyone else, and followed Finn out the door.

He took off at a decent pace and I had to quicken my step to keep up. I cast one final look over my shoulder, back toward the house, but there was no telling from the outside that anything weird was going on behind the old, cladded walls. The sensation of discomfort that had hung heavy in the room now clung to my skin, and it wasn't easy to shake it off. I couldn't understand why I should feel both reluctant and relieved to leave those beautiful, baffling people behind.

It usually took me a full twenty minutes to walk to school, but I did it every day unless the weather was bad. I could have taken a shorter, duller route through the neighborhood, but I always chose to detour through the bushland. The walk was nice, sure, but what I appreciated more was the extra delay it added to the start of my day.

It was impossible to concentrate on the hike and keep up a conversation at the same time, so Finn and I crunched our way over the dry leaves in companionable silence, emerging from the trees at what was the unmarked border of the school grounds. By then, my thoughts had snarled up nice and tight, and I was busting to ask Finn why he'd been so weird with Grams's visitors.

"What was that all about?" I demanded.

"What was what all about?"

"The way you behaved with those people. You were upset."

"I misread the situation, that's all."

I had no reason to doubt him, but Finn's answer was a little superficial. I tried again, hunting for something with more juice to it.

"Not the normal crowd for Grams's Monday group, are they?"

He gave me a wry look. "Since when have Grams or Harry been known for being *normal*? It's more of the same, Rae. I bet the new guys bail soon, anyway."

"Why would you think that?"

"They didn't seem very happy to be here," he pointed out.

He was right. Nobody seemed happy to be in that room today. I chewed my lip as I turned Finn's words over in my head, but nothing new occurred to me in the minute or so I had to spare before we reached the school buildings.

I judged the distance between us and the campus—thirty seconds at this pace, max—and then pointedly eyed Finn's tanned, muscled arms, on show because he'd chosen to wear a sleeveless shirt today.

"Since when is *that* considered appropriate attire for school?" I asked archly, nodding in the direction of his chest.

He laughed and swung his backpack around so he could fish out a clean shirt. He dropped his bag and I stopped too, so I could watch him peel away his damp tank top.

Yes, okay, fine. Most of the time, I totally judged all those girls who'd murder their best friends to score a date with Finn O'Brien, but some days I had to count myself among them. He was that glorious.

"Checking out the abs?" he teased with a knowing chuckle.

"You wish," I retorted, flushing scarlet and shoving against his chest. My feeble attack didn't budge him an inch, and he laughed harder.

I rolled my eyes and stomped away. Finn caught up to me quickly, slinging his heavy arm over my shoulder and pulling me into his side so we were walking almost on top of each other. He smelled like soap and clean sweat, and the heat of his body felt nice, even with the humidity in the air, but his teasing had embarrassed me, so I shrugged him off and lengthened my stride.

"Okay, I'll see you at lunch then!" he called brightly, ignoring my pique as I took off to my first class.

He knew exactly how to infuriate me, and I didn't reply.

Some days, I didn't know if I wanted to date Finn because I was too busy trying not to kill him.

Dreamer's Log: Margaret
Day Eleven of October, Year 1666

A year and a day have passed since the Master of Fear was felled in body but not in spirit, yet I have seen not a hint of him in the dream. Oh, I know he lurks there, peeking in, right on the edges where hell begins.

I am certain of the reason he has abandoned his body. He lingers in the aether, leering from the shadows as was always his way, pained and driven mad with the need to recover his magic. Better for him that he reclaims it before waking, for without it he has no power on this mortal coil.

I suspect that one or more of his foul demonic creations has hidden his corpse and even now readies it against the return of his spirit. I'm sure they await their master's resurrection with bated, blooded breath! But I keep faith that before that day comes, I will confront him in the dream and, using the very magic he so desperately desires for himself, I will vanquish him for all eternity.

I return to the pouch at random, only when I am not watched and never in the same month twice. The wards hold fast, and I would know the instant they had been breached. I've had no reason to doubt my plan and will go on as I have always done until given good cause to diverge.

I wished to never have to do this, but at the next new moon, I will guide Kateryn to the magic, and have her reset the wards under my direction. I have resisted her impatience for as long as I can, and I fear she will begin to venture on her own if I do not agree to share the secret immediately.

Have I waited too long to teach her? She is strong in the dream but not a young woman anymore. I cannot tell if her strength will be enough.

CHAPTER TWO

I slumped into the chair opposite Principal Peskin's desk, my legs sprawled in front of me and my head lolling back as I tried to make shapes out of the water stains on the ceiling. The office assistant had sent me in to wait, but it had already been five minutes, and I was only going to give him five more before I left. This was my lunch hour, after all.

With ninety seconds left before his deadline, the door clicked open and I sat up straight. I guessed I wouldn't be getting out of here so easily after all.

"Miss Quinn," he greeted me, exhaustion dragging down his tone. How could he be tired already? It was the first day back, for crying out loud.

"Mr. Peskin," I replied, not quite mocking his serious mood, but coming close.

He lowered himself into his big leather chair and stared at me over steepled fingers. I stared back.

"Riley," he said eventually, dropping his arms and leaning back. "Did you find any time over the break to think more about the accelerated learning program we discussed last year?"

I knew it.

"It's not for me, sir," I said, not for the first time.

"You might enjoy it," he argued, also not for the first time. "You coast through your classes, and you're always at the top of your grade. You have so much *potential*, Riley. I'd hate to see it go to waste."

"The only waste would be to give this opportunity to me instead of someone who actually wants it."

He shook his head, disappointment turning down the corners of his mouth. "And your grandmother—what does she say?"

"Grams wants what I want," I hedged.

"Riley, you have a *gift*. Don't turn your back on it."

"I'm not turning my back on anything," I disagreed, standing and heaving my bag onto my back. This was a dead-end conversation. "I know what's important, and what's not."

"Riley, please." The principal knew as well as I did there was no way he was going to change my mind, and right then I felt a little bad for him.

"Thanks, Mr. Peskin," I said, turning for the exit. "I'll see you around."

I shut the door behind me before he could say goodbye.

"So, that wasn't too bad, was it?"

Finn walked alongside me as we finally left the old

brown-brick school buildings behind us and tramped over the playing fields toward the trees. He'd already traded his administration-sanctioned shorts and shirt for the board shorts and tank top rolled up in his bag, but he still wore sneakers on his feet. Flip-flops weren't hardy enough for hiking.

"It wasn't too good either," I replied.

"Only a year to go, Rae, then you'll never have to step foot in this place again."

"Hallelujah," I said flatly.

Finn snorted.

I cut away toward the east side of the fields, heading for the stretch of walking track that would deliver me home. To my surprise, Finn followed.

"Do you want to come over today?" I asked.

"Is that okay?"

"Sure. It's just a little odd, for a Monday." I paused, and when it seemed he hadn't caught on to my meaning, I clarified my confusion. "Gram's group, remember? I can't guarantee it'll be over by now."

Finn swung his foot to kick a large rock out of his way, and then bent down to pick up a slender branch, which he used as a walking staff.

"I think I'll come anyway," he said eventually.

"Suits me. It'll be nice to have you there. I hate Mondays."

He grunted his agreement but said nothing about the strangers. I suspected he was as curious as I was.

"Rae? What are you going to do next year? School will be over, and…I don't know. I've been wondering about your plans."

I looked at him in surprise, but he was walking with his head down, concentrating on the ground under his feet. I tore my eyes away before he could look up. Finn could read me too well, and he'd register the panic creasing my forehead.

I couldn't recall a time Finn had ever asked me questions about my future, and we never talked about the "what next?" in our lives. Tomorrow had always been some far-off thing and we were totally happy living in the moment. At least, I thought we were. I could and would and did talk to Finn about almost anything—our screwed-up families and our fears we'd end up just like them, the people we loved and those we missed—hell, I'd trust him with my life—but his tone was too loaded to for this to qualify as one of those conversations.

Had Mr. Peskin talked to Finn? The thought of the principal and my best friend discussing my education behind my back left me seething.

"I don't know, Finn. Join the circus?" I retorted.

"Be serious, Rae. Haven't you thought about it at all?"

I shrugged irritably and deflected. Offense was the best defense. "Have you?"

"I've thought about it a lot. That's why I'm asking. I want to be wherever you are."

I was relieved we were walking while talking, our focus

divided between the words we were speaking and where we placed our feet so we wouldn't trip. My heart had taken off and my hands tingled, and meeting his eyes at this point would only make things worse.

Why did he *do* this?

Finn had a habit of saying things that sounded significant, but he never meant anything by them. He loved me like a best friend or, worse, a *sister*. I squirmed whenever our conversations teetered on the edge of potential misunderstanding, a traitorous part of me hoping that this time, it would be different.

"Am I that irresistible?" I joked, trying to lighten the mood. I was rewarded when a splotchy blush crept up his neck, but it also reminded me, yet again, that Finn was never going to think of me *that way*. It mortified him when I teased him like that.

I sighed and returned to his question reluctantly. "I guess I'll hang around here until I work out a plan."

From the corner of my eye, I saw him nod. "We've got a year to figure it out. You're going to do great things, Rae. We just need to decide what those things are going to be."

I had no idea why Finn had such faith in me, or why he thought I'd be the one doing "great things" while he followed me around in the role of World's Best-Looking Cheerleader. There was no way I could live up to his high standards and besides, I wanted more for him than that, regardless of where I ended up. In my gloomiest hours, I couldn't imagine either of us ever leaving this town, but it didn't feel like the right time to say so.

"We'll see," I said to placate him.

"We will," he said, his good humor returned. "And in the meantime, we can talk about Lizzie Porter."

"Oh, no," I groaned. "What now?"

Lizzie Porter was Finn O'Brien's *number one fan!* She'd pursued him relentlessly ever since her hormones had kicked in in the eighth grade, and had orchestrated any number of "accidental" hook-ups over the years—group dates where everyone else conveniently bailed at the last minute, party games of spin the bottle that wouldn't end until she'd kissed him, coincidental meetings at the beach, at the corner store, anywhere Finn might be on the weekends. Lizzie hadn't gone so far as to meet the official definition of *stalker*, but she wasn't far off.

Finn never complained about it, and he rebuffed her advances with his trademark charm. I'd expect no less from him, but it meant that Lizzie never got the hint. He'd never taken her up on her offers and there had been four years' worth of them, so I genuinely believed he didn't like her *that* way, but her behavior bothered me on his behalf.

I wondered why the girl had so little self-respect. Didn't she think she deserved a guy who liked her back? Lizzie was annoying but pretty and smart enough, and any of the boys in our senior year would have loved to date her, but her sights were set firmly on Finn.

"She's the chairperson for this year's formal committee," Finn said, a grin splitting his face as he told me the story. "She's trying to make it girls' choice, with the condition that the boy can't say no. The committee voted and it's split right down the middle, so now she has to convince everyone it's a great idea or Mrs. Lopez will make the final decision, and you know she'll say no."

Finn flashed his wide smile as he anticipated my reaction.

"She's got no shame!" I spluttered. "Finn, come on! Hasn't this gone on long enough? You need to set her straight. This is our final year, and she's going to try every trick in the book to land you before we graduate."

"Lizzie's not so bad," Finn replied evenly. "It's not my fault she's desperately in love with me."

He was being deliberately obtuse, and something in his attitude flicked a cog in my brain.

"You like it, don't you?" I exclaimed, stumbling over a bump in the ground. He reached out to steady me, and his crooked smirk confirmed my suspicions. "You're unbelievable! You love having Lizzie Porter running after you, making you feel all gorgeous and wonderful. Ugh! That's horrible."

Finn laughed, the chuckles reverberating deep in his chest. "It's not all bad," he admitted, eyeing me sideways. "And why do you care so much? Are you jealous or something?"

"Four years of Lizzie's love notes have gone to your head," I fired back. "You need me, Finn, to keep your ego in check. Not everyone thinks you're God's gift to women, you know."

"Aw, thanks, Rae," he said, reaching over to pat me on the head. I ducked out of his way indignantly. "You always know what to say to make a guy feel good about himself."

I gave him my best glare. "And don't you forget it."

We finally reached the house, passing the same cars I'd noticed on the drive that morning—a sleek silver coupe and a bright white Range Rover. My heart skipped a beat at the thought of who might still be inside. I opened the front door and warily stepped in, Finn right behind me. I dropped my schoolbag onto the floor and braced myself.

They were all still in the room, sitting in the same chairs, standing in the same positions, giving the unnerving impression that no time had passed in the last seven hours.

"Ah, hi, Grams, and everyone," I said uneasily, regretting that I'd paused in the hall.

I didn't usually stop to say hello. On Mondays, I barreled through the house with my head down, determined to avoid even a suggestion of interest in Grams's activities, but today I couldn't help myself. I couldn't walk past these strange, stunningly pretty people without taking another look.

Finn didn't so much as glance into the room before he took my hand and roughly pulled at it.

"Let's get something to eat and hide out upstairs," he said. "Let these guys talk shop, or whatever it is they do here."

"Okay," I agreed, thankful he'd given me an excuse to keep moving, but Grams spoke before we could complete our escape.

"Riley, Finn, please wait."

She looked at Harry, raising her eyebrows in an unspoken question, but he shook his head a little and tugged at his nose. Grams then directed her expression at Perry.

The strange man nodded. "I have another son, and a daughter, who will start at the high school tomorrow," he explained. "Seth is your age and in his final year. His sister, Felicity, is a year younger. And there's also Adeline's brother, Van, who will join you."

I stared at the man's mouth, again bemused by the shape of his words, the sounds on his lips. The room was still, everyone waiting for a response, and the silence stretched.

"Super," Finn finally replied, not even pretending to care.

Harry gave Finn an admonishing look, which he blatantly ignored. Instead, he hauled me to the kitchen, where I watched him raid the fridge. Satisfied with two ham-and-cheese sandwiches, three apples, a chunk of leftover carrot cake, and a half-empty bottle of orange juice, he carefully stowed his goods under an arm, in his pockets, and on one hand, and used the other to drag me up the stairs.

When we reached my tiny bedroom, Finn set his snacks on my desk and closed the door. He hooked his smartphone into my speakers and turned up the volume on his playlist. Only then did he collapse on my unmade bed, grabbing a sandwich on the way.

I stared at him, thinking, and he pretended not to notice my scrutiny. He seemed relaxed, demolishing his food the way he always did, but something felt off—about Grams's friends, about Harry's reticence, about Finn's behavior, about all of it.

"What do you think about these new kids starting school with us tomorrow?" I asked casually, noisily biting into one of the apples.

Finn shrugged. "We'll avoid them. It won't be hard if they look anything like those guys. Who do they think they are?" He laughed, but it sounded sharp. "I'll bet you twenty dollars the whole lot of them leave town before the end of the month. They're going to hate it here." He handed me his smartphone. "Here, choose another song."

It took superhuman strength not to voice the retort that balanced on my lips.

There's something you're not telling me.

I didn't think these new strangers were going anywhere and I knew Finn didn't think so either. But in the end, I said nothing. I took his phone and dropped the subject, but my thoughts continued to drift in the direction of the visitors downstairs.

Dreamer's Log: Margaret
Day Twenty-Two of December, Year 1667

Oh, he is a monster! I walk the dream every night, and too often the skin between my shoulder blades itches with the touch of his eyes. The devil ever hovers at the perimeter of my mind, never advancing. He knows better than to enter my head uninvited!

More than once, I have considered using the magic as a lure, to tempt him to take my dream by force. Ah, to have him steal my mind without consent! Then I could destroy him completely and be done with this painful wait! But no, I dare not risk it. And so, it goes on.

Demons of the dream have begun to harry us. Is this at their master's bidding, or can the incubi sense something of the magic we protect? I do not know the answers yet.

I confess that my hope this would be all done while I lived is starting to wear thin, for there is sickness in my body. And so, this dangerous task may yet fall to Kateryn, though it breaks my heart to know it and be helpless to make it otherwise.

Even so, I have great pride in the dreamer she is and one day will be, for her strength of spirit is great, and continues to grow almost daily.

Just last month I forced myself to stand aside while she lay in wait for the incubus who thought to try himself against her. She felt his approach in the dream, as did I, and it was all I could do to watch without acting, my stomach in my throat, as my girl did battle with this most vile of vampiric creatures. He thought to kill her—and, of course, found himself thoroughly dead by the end of it.

CHAPTER THREE

Finn stayed all afternoon, until about six o'clock when Grams's meeting finally finished. I heard the bustling noises of the strangers leaving but Finn didn't mention it, so I didn't either, and soon after that Harry knocked on my bedroom door. He opened it without waiting for my invitation.

"Okay, party's over," he rumbled. "It's time to go, Finn."

"Good timing. I'm starved," Finn replied.

Finn gathered up his things and, not for the first time, I wondered at the fact that neither my Grams nor Finn's dad had a problem with the two of us hiding ourselves behind closed doors. You'd think responsible adults would make rules about that sort of thing, but neither seemed to worry about what we might have been up to when no one was watching.

Everyone knew Finn was a catch, so I tried not to think too much about what that said about me.

"I'll see you in school tomorrow," I said to Finn in the way of a goodbye.

"Meet you here at eight," he countered.

"Here?"

"Sure, why not? I don't know why we hike through the bush from opposite directions every morning. It makes more sense to start at the same place."

"You live on the other side of town, so it *makes sense* to meet at school," I argued.

"Don't sleep in," he said, ignoring me. "I don't want to have to wait for you."

I threw my apple core at him, and he smoothly snatched it out of the air. He smiled in satisfaction at the speed of his own reflexes, and I gave him one of my world-famous eye-rolls.

"Safe dreams, Riley," Harry offered, ushering Finn from the room. "Finn'll see you bright and early."

"Bye, Harry," I replied, watching the two men—Finn now with shoulders bigger than his father's—navigate the narrow hall outside my room. As soon as they cleared the landing, Grams appeared in the bedroom doorway. She smiled at me, but her eyes were distant.

"Everything okay?" I asked.

"Of course," she said. "Never better. I was just thinking about dinner. Will you help me in the kitchen?"

We headed for our compact cooking station, complete with a two-burner stove over a small oven. Grams was a good cook, which meant I was learning to be one too, because her gnarly fingers wouldn't let her chop and stir as she once had. Instead, she gave me orders and supervised the pans, and chatted to me while I did the work. I'd grown attached to the comforting routine, and I liked knowing that the break from preparing food rested Grams's hands so she could continue her silver craft.

Tonight, however, as I followed her painfully slow footsteps down the stairs, I was distracted by how small she'd become, how delicate. How *old.* I helped her settle into one of the two chairs at our dining table, and then opened the refrigerator.

"What'll it be?" I asked.

"Whatever you like," Grams replied. "I don't have too much of an appetite tonight."

My vague thoughts over her well-being bubbled into concern. "Grams, do you feel okay?"

She waved away my worry, and I was reminded that she may have been old, but I'd never met anyone tougher. "I'm fine. It's just been an exciting day."

This was my shot to ask about today's visitors, and I didn't hesitate. "Who were those people, Grams? They were a little…different."

I made a show of scanning the contents of the fridge, but my attention was entirely on Grams's answer.

"They are…different," she agreed.

"Is that a bad thing?"

"If different were a bad thing, I'd be in serious trouble," Grams replied with a small laugh, but then she sighed, her focus directed inward. "But in this case, I'm not sure yet."

I flung shut the refrigerator door and rounded on her.

"Grams, what do you mean? Are these people dangerous?"

I had never believed my great-grandmother's obsession with superstition was more than silly nonsense, just the eccentricities of an unusual old woman. Now, I was concerned her hobbies had attracted the attention of people who took these things more seriously. Perhaps Grams was in over her head. This odd family might be too strange, even for her standards.

"Riley, sit with me for a moment," Grams said, reaching out to pat the table in front of the empty chair. The old wooden seat creaked as I fell into it, and I clenched my hands nervously in my lap.

"Grams, what's going on? You're worrying me."

"I don't mean to do that," Grams said, shaking her head. "I'm a foolish old woman, and I should know how to handle this better." She shifted and sighed again. "These newcomers are unusual, but they share my *superstitions*, as you call them." Grams raised an amused eyebrow in my direction. She was well aware of my feelings on this subject, and she tolerated my skepticism with patience, just as I tolerated her unconventional ideologies with barely concealed frustration. "They are fellow believers," she went on, "but their practice is a little different from ours. Same theory, alternative interpretations, you could say. We disagree on certain key points."

I threw up my hands, irritation burning away the cold fear that a moment ago had frozen my blood. "Grams, if you're going to tell me this is all about a difference of *opinions* on the merits of silver versus steel, or how best to tell a person's fortune, or whether vampires are coming for us in the night, I think I'll scream. You're too old to believe this crap and now you've landed yourself in hot water by attracting the wrong kind of people—people who look like they take these things a little too seriously."

I scowled at her, refusing to feel guilty about losing my temper. Grams's fingers fidgeted on the tabletop. Her mouth opened, and then closed. Then she straightened her back and looked me directly in the eyes, and the glimmer of guilt disappeared completely.

Grams had never had an argument she couldn't win.

"Yes," she said stubbornly. "That's exactly what I'm telling you. There's a very great difference of opinion, but they're fellow believers, nonetheless. I don't like some of their ideas, and I told them as much today."

I groaned. "Grams, can't you bite your tongue occasionally?"

"I bite my tongue often enough," she replied testily. "But I'll always speak my mind when it's important."

I refrained from observing out loud that her idea of what was and was not important was highly subjective—and she could never read the room. Instead, I said, "So I suppose I should expect things to be awkward tomorrow, when the new kids start at school."

"Don't trouble yourself with Perry's children," Grams

replied. "To tell the truth, I'd prefer it if you kept your distance."

Grams had never interfered with my social life before, not that I had much going for me in that arena, so her comment surprised me.

"You don't want me to be friends with them?" I asked.

"I think they'll be happier left to their own devices," Grams replied.

"Finn thinks they won't stay long. He says the whole family will leave town sooner rather than later."

"I think young Finn is wrong on that point," Grams disagreed. "My prediction is they'll be here for a while yet."

I could think of nothing to say to that, and I wasn't about to admit that I sensed the truth in Grams's words, but Grams watched me thoughtfully, as though she could read my mind.

I shrugged in an effort to seem disinterested. "I'll worry about it tomorrow," I said. "Are you sure you're not hungry? There's enough leftover casserole for two."

"I think I'll turn in early," she said. "There's some reading I'd like to do."

I watched as Grams pushed herself onto her feet and shuffled her way up the stairs. More for something to do than to satisfy any real hunger, I put a small portion of the casserole into the oven to warm through. I showered quickly and felt pleasantly refreshed after the spray of cool water. With wet hair hanging down my back and dampening my cotton pajamas, I finally sat down with my food.

Sitting there alone, the house still and quiet, my thoughts returned to the beautiful strangers. Perry had been polite enough. Leo and Noel were attractive, and Adeline even more so. I had thought at the time the woman had taken an instant dislike to me but, knowing what I did now, I wondered if Adeline's problem wasn't so much with me as it was with my great-grandmother.

Grams had as good as ordered me to stay away from the new kids, and Finn had said we'd simply avoid them. Being told what I should do irked me no end, but I couldn't think of a good enough reason to argue with either of them. After twenty minutes spent deliberating over my bowl of chicken and vegetables, my final plan was a simple one. I'd give Seth, Felicity, and Van as much of my attention as I gave to any of Grams's friends—which was none at all.

Putting the problem out of my mind, I cleaned my dinner plate and returned to my room. I attached my phone to the speakers so I could listen to music while I did my homework, and was reminded of my discussion with Principal Peskin, followed by the questions Finn had asked me that afternoon. I shoved my textbooks back into my bag, all motivation completely quashed. I didn't want to think about life after graduation then, and I didn't want to think about it now.

I knew I needed to come up with a way to make a living when I was no longer a student and, no matter what Finn believed, higher education wasn't in the cards. Just because a person found learning easy didn't mean they wanted to do more of it than they absolutely had to.

And I couldn't leave Grams. I couldn't seriously think about finding my own place or moving away, and she'd provided for me for long enough, so my only priority had to be making enough money to take care of us both.

The next song on my playlist was deep and dark, the lyrics slow and depressing. When I recognized the opening notes, I lunged at the cue to indulge my lousy mood, crashing onto the bed and closing my eyes to better feel into the music.

Though we fought as often as we laughed, I really did try my best to remain even-tempered around Grams. After the hell she went through with my mother, I never wanted to give her a reason to worry that she'd have to raise another rebellious, unreasonable teenager, especially at her age, but I often felt like one.

I took a few deep breaths, trying and failing to calm my irritation, and again my mind wandered in the direction of Perry's family. I recalled their names, their faces, the few words I'd heard them speak. I wondered if the younger ones would share the pale beauty, black eyes, and unusual energy of their older siblings. I imagined what I might do if I was forced by circumstance to talk to them, perhaps about a homework assignment or to give them directions to the library. I worried a little about what would happen when Finn came face to face with them.

Eventually, I fell asleep. I never dreamed—which I'd

always thought was ironic given Grams was obsessed with the meanings of dreams and protecting mine from the whims of demonic prowlers—but that night I felt like my imagination was trying to show me pictures while I slept. Colors and shapes and sounds teased the edges of my vision and prevented me from sinking into a deep slumber, so I tossed and turned until the sun came up.

Dreamer's Log: Kateryn (daughter of Margaret)
Day Four of June, Year 1671

I was walking alone when he approached me in the twilight hours, and I knew at once what he was. My body quivered with fear and attraction, as Mama had told me it would. Oh, he was beautiful!

He asked for my consent, but I knew better than to give it, so of course he took my dream by force. It was an uncomfortable sensation, my dreams opened to another against my will, but it was easy enough to soothe that hurt.

As I've done but once before, and then under the guidance of my mother, I turned upon the incubus instantly, and embraced the power that scorched my veins. His arrogance made him slow—not that speed could have saved him!—and he knew not what had happened before it was done. Of that I am certain, for he was dead before his eyes blinked twice.

CHAPTER FOUR

We were two hours into the school day and all anyone wanted to talk about was the new kids.

I hadn't seen them up close yet, though I had spied them from a distance, disappearing around a corner as they walked to first-period classes. They stood out, and not only because of the long, dark clothes they wore like uniforms. People walked wide of them, heads turning as they passed.

I listened attentively but, I hoped, inconspicuously to the gossip, and nothing I heard surprised me. By all accounts, our new schoolmates were too odd to blend in.

Finn and I were on our way to our third-period classes when Lizzie Porter sidled up on Finn's other side.

"Hey, Lizzie," Finn greeted her.

"Hey, Finn," she replied in her high, chirpy voice. "Have you seen the new kids yet?"

"Nope," Finn said shortly, his lips popping on the "p."

I eyed him sideways. Nobody but me knew him well enough to pick up the sharp edge in his voice. Lizzie missed it entirely.

"Just wait until you do," she said, her eyes widening. "I've never seen anyone like them. There are two boys, both in our year, and a girl, a year younger. They're so…so…weird."

"Oh, yeah?" Inexplicably, Finn now sounded like he actually cared. "How's that?"

I tried to read my best friend's face without giving myself away. Why the sudden interest?

"You need to see them for yourself," Lizzie replied breathily.

I peeked around Finn's broad chest to get a better look at Lizzie, but she snubbed me completely, occupied instead with running her fingers through her long blonde hair.

Lizzie and I were not friends, nor were we exactly enemies. I disliked her because she was irritating. She disliked me because I was Finn's closest friend and an exasperating inconvenience—not quite a rival, not quite irrelevant.

"Freaks, are they?" Finn teased.

"Not exactly," Lizzie replied slowly. "Just…*strange*. They're so pale—paler than Riley, I swear. They wear these fancy dark clothes—long pants, long shirts—and they all look the same, but only Seth and Felicity Callaghan are related. Van Bennet, the other one, is Felicity's boyfriend."

"So, what makes them so weird?"

Lizzie sighed. "They're so *beautiful*."

Finn snorted.

"Well, they are," Lizzie said, pouting a little and clutching her textbooks against her chest. "Like models or something.

They act like them, too—so unfriendly. I tried to talk to Seth—the tall one—but he brushed me off."

Finn's voice turned hard. "Stay away from them, Lizzie. Forget all about them."

Lizzie smiled as though she'd won a prize. "You're right," she agreed. "Thanks, Finn."

Finn and I left Lizzie at the science labs for her biology lesson. When we were out of earshot, I elbowed Finn hard in the ribs.

"What was that all about?" I demanded.

"Ow!" he replied, avoiding my eyes. "What?"

"Twenty questions about the new kids," I hissed. "Why do you care?"

"I don't," he said. "I was making small talk. It's the polite thing to do."

"And why do you care if Lizzie wants to be friends with them? What business is it of yours?"

"I don't care," he argued. "I was being nice."

Something about the way Finn danced around the subject was odd, and suddenly I understood. "Do you *like* Lizzie Porter?" I spluttered.

"What? No!"

I wanted to believe him, but a flush stained his cheeks and I wished I could start over. If Finn liked Lizzie—if the idea of her being friendly to the new guy made him jealous—I shouldn't have made him feel uncomfortable about admitting it.

"Finn, I'm sorry. You can talk to me about it…if you want to." He was silent, so I added a little white lie. "I like Lizzie. You two look great together."

"I don't *like* Lizzie, okay?"

"But if you did—," I began.

"You'd be the first to know," he finished brusquely.

He still wasn't looking at me, and I couldn't shake the feeling I'd missed something important in our conversation, but I'd already done enough damage, so I cut my losses and distracted him with questions about basketball instead.

I met Seth Callaghan for the first time in the lunch hour.

Finn was running late, so I sat alone in our usual spot, on a fallen log under the trees on the far side of campus, resisting the urge to eat without him. I was idly watching the people around me, paying no attention to anyone in particular, when I saw the new kids exit the west building.

They were together, the three of them, dressed in various but dark styles of tight denim jeans, long linen shirts, and expensive sneakers, and they moved with identical grace. I watched them with anxious curiosity.

They didn't appear to speak to one another before Seth separated from the others. I knew it was him because he was taller than the other boy, and the shorter one held the girl's hand, which made him Van Bennet, Felicity's boyfriend.

Those two watched Seth for a moment as he walked away, and then they turned and disappeared around a corner.

Seth moved at a steady pace, gaining ground quickly without appearing to rush. I marveled at the way he walked—confidently, with his broad shoulders back and his legs covering the ground with long strides. Soon, he was close enough for me to make out his features in more detail, and I marveled at those, too—thick dark brows over brooding black eyes, the lines of his face fine enough to be called pretty if it weren't for his strong, muscular jaw. His hair, thick and tousled, was almost black, but the sun exposed its warmer colors as it glinted in the light. His mouth quirked up at one corner, as though he recalled something amusing.

Lizzie hadn't overstated his beauty. This boy was unearthly.

Too late, I realized he was coming closer. I twisted around to look for potential attractions, unable to understand where he was going.

Too late, I realized he was walking to me.

Seth paused a few steps away from where I sat. The sun shone overhead, and I squinted up at him. A million tiny vibrations buzzed insistently under my skin.

"Hello," he said politely. "I'm Seth Callaghan."

My mouth felt suddenly dry.

"I know," I replied, instantly wishing I could have the words back.

He flashed a small smile but all he said was, "And you're Riley Quinn."

"I know," I repeated.

I sounded like an idiot. It was his face, I thought. Too distracting.

"May I sit with you?" he asked.

"Okay," I said, sliding over to make room.

He settled himself on the edge of the fallen log. "I hope you don't mind my introducing myself. I felt comfortable saying hello because we're already acquainted, in a manner of speaking."

I tried to concentrate on what Seth was saying, but his mouth demanded too much of my attention. I stared, transfixed, as his pale pink lips shaped each word, and as they left his tongue with soft soothing sounds. I leaned in, fascinated, and his mouth curved into that amused smile.

"Riley?" he said gently.

"Yes?" I whispered.

"Are you okay?"

I blinked deliberately, pulling back and dragging my eyes away from his face, focusing instead on the ground underneath my feet. That seemed to help.

"I'm fine. I'm just…fine, thanks."

The key seemed to be not looking directly at him. Kind of like the sun.

"I didn't mean to bother you."

"You're not bothering me," I replied.

"I'm glad. Are you having a good day?"

"Uh, sure?"

I forgot myself and looked at him again, but he was staring into the distance. I took the opportunity to examine his profile. It was flawless, all chiseled lines, but this angle didn't scramble my wits as much.

"Are *you* having a good day?" I asked, taking advantage of my ability to think coherently again.

"We didn't share any classes this morning," he pointed out, not answering my question.

"No, we didn't."

"What's your schedule like for this afternoon?"

My schedule? My schedule. I begged my brain to work faster, and finally pulled my Tuesday classes from my memory.

"History, then economics."

He smiled with what looked like satisfaction, and I took note of his straight white teeth. "Perhaps it will be a good day after all," he said, turning his face toward me again.

I swallowed nervously and nodded.

He tilted his head as he considered me. "Riley, do you think we can be friends?"

"You want to be my friend?" I asked, surprised.

"I do."

"Why?" I blurted out.

"Why not?"

I couldn't bring myself to tell him Grams had asked me not to socialize with him. I didn't want to tell him I'd made a deal with my best friend to avoid him.

Seth watched me with dark, patient eyes, waiting for

an answer. The silence had stretched too long so I spoke without thinking.

"Sure. Friends."

He grinned but said nothing.

"Are you settling in okay?" I asked, social conditioning compelling me to fill the silence.

"You could say that, but we actually arrived in town more than a month ago."

"Oh. I didn't know that."

"You weren't supposed to," he said, that amused curve returning to his mouth. "We prefer to keep to ourselves."

"So, why—"

He stood abruptly, staring toward the west building, where Felicity and Van had reappeared. They were obviously waiting for Seth because they faced our direction, watching us. Seth looked down at me.

"It was nice talking to you, Riley."

"It was nice talking to you too, Seth." It felt awkward to say his name, but I enjoyed the sound of it, and the feel of it on my lips.

"Nice earrings, by the way," he said, and then he walked away with that long, confident stride.

I watched him leave, appreciating his beauty from an entirely new angle. As the distance between us grew, the buzzing under my skin gradually faded away, and I distractedly registered the relaxing of muscles I hadn't noticed were tensed. Wild horses couldn't have dragged my attention away from his retreating figure, so I watched until he rejoined Felicity and Van, and they all disappeared again.

Once he was no longer monopolizing my awareness, I realized I'd been fiddling with the jewelry on my ear, and that the kids at the other end of the field were staring at me. Some exchanged whispers, and one even pointed. I grimaced. It appeared my exchange with the mysterious new kid hadn't gone unnoticed.

"What did he want?"

I jumped as Finn stepped over the fallen tree trunk from behind me, dropped his bag on the ground, and sat down. His face was flushed, and his hair was dark with sweat. He must have stayed behind in his P.E. class.

"Seth?" I asked, playing for time.

"Who else?"

"He wanted to say hello, I guess," I replied evasively.

"And?"

"And that's it. Hello. Goodbye. He mentioned Grams. Maybe he thinks we have some things in common."

Finn snorted. "You've got nothing in common with that guy."

"Well, that's not exactly true. His father and Grams share a few similarities—"

"Did he ask you for anything?"

I paused, unsure about what to tell him. Finn already seemed agitated, and I didn't want to complicate things more than they already were.

"Rae?" Finn demanded again. "Did he want something from you?"

"No. What would he want from me?"

"Nothing. It doesn't matter." Finn shook his head and reached into his schoolbag for his lunch.

I understood why Finn wanted nothing to do with Seth or his family. When it came to the people in Grams's group, we did our best to not get caught up in the nonsense. It made it harder that Finn's entire family was into it, but the two of us had managed to remain relatively normal when everyone around us was flipping out about walking nightmares and magic silver bullets. We were a team, Finn and me, and I couldn't risk that, so I didn't tell him that Seth had asked me to be his friend, or that I'd said yes.

Dreamer's Log: Brigid (daughter of Kateryn)
Day Ten of October, Year 1695

I often reread the dream logs of my grandmother, searching for a hint, by word or omission, of when she thought this trial might end, but I can only deduce that she had no inkling we'd still be anticipating the devil's revival some thirty years after his death.

What would I tell her, were she here today? Perhaps, "Grandmother, the king of hell haunts all my sleeping hours. I sense his presence as hot, foul breath at the nape of my neck. Silly me. I always imagine my hair loose and long when I walk the dream, so I do not take fancies that it is, indeed, his mouth at my back. It is all in my imagination, I am sure, for I have not ever actually seen him."

I mark the date now to commemorate three long decades since the Master of Fear was struck through the heart, his body ended, his soul banished to the aether. And three long decades that the women of our family have stood guard over his magic, ready to finish him forever.

And Mother! You had thought to be done with this duty long since, and still we wait! I wish you were here. How I miss you, as does dear Agnes, that strange daughter of mine. She is a powerful dreamer but so fiery of character. We argue often, and many of her ideas are unconventional, but I must believe her headstrong nature will hold her in good stead should she be the one destined to face and fell our enemy.

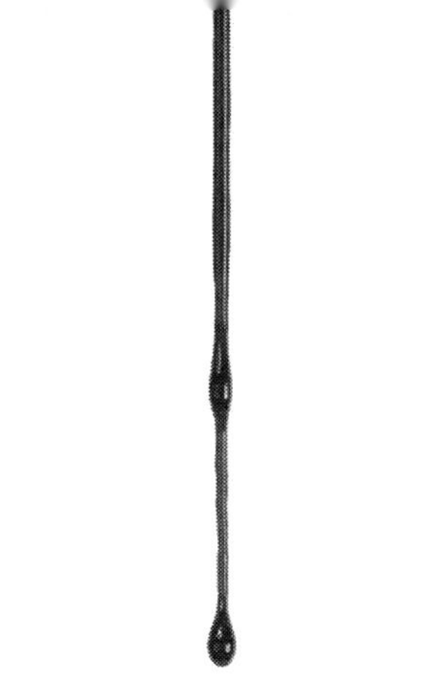

CHAPTER FIVE

I walked into my history lesson, and my heart jumped clear into my throat.

Seth sat alone at a desk at the back of the room. His head lifted as I stepped through the doorway, and our eyes met for the briefest second while I hesitated, revising my premeditation to take the desk under the window. In ordinary circumstances, a person would choose to join someone she considered a friend rather than sit by herself—but these weren't ordinary circumstances.

I looked back at him, and he smiled.

I'd crossed the room before I knew where my feet were taking me.

"May I sit here?"

I couldn't recall the last time I'd been this nervous—certainly never over a boy—and I was annoyed that I sounded breathless. The insistent buzz in my body was back.

"Of course," he said, shifting his books to make room for mine.

I slid into the empty chair next to him and couldn't help

it. I looked at him. Perhaps I'd braced myself well enough because the impact of his face wasn't as decimating as it had been at lunch, and my heart only constricted a little. To be safe, I quickly looked away again, and watched the rest of the class arrive in twos and threes.

Nearly every eye flickered our way as people took note that Riley Quinn was sitting next to the strange new boy. I very deliberately ignored them.

"Do you like this class?" Seth asked politely.

In truth, I didn't mind it. I objected more to the institution of school—the rules, the exams, the expectations—than I did the content. I enjoyed reading as much as the challenge of a difficult math problem, and I had a good memory. Mr. Peskin had been right about one thing—it didn't take much for me to maintain my A-grade average, in this or any of my classes. The irony of it wasn't lost on me. My brains would have been better given to someone who actually cared about doing something with them.

"I do," I replied.

"But?" he pressed, perhaps sensing that I'd given him an incomplete answer.

"I don't like school," I admitted.

"You don't?"

He sounded surprised, so I looked directly at him. His face was open and curious.

"Too many rules. Too many standards. Too many ways to fit too many people into not enough boxes."

He chuckled.

"What?" I demanded, my face heating with embarrassment.

"You're not what I expected," he said, shaking his head. "I thought Maggie Quinn's great-granddaughter would be like Maggie Quinn, and the earrings seem to back up that theory, but when we arrived in town, Maggie told us you were nothing like her, and that you've completely rejected her way of life."

"She told you that?"

It shouldn't have surprised me that Grams had shared her opinion so transparently with practical strangers—Grams had no filter—but it did.

Seth seemed to notice my discomfort because his next words were delivered with a smile. "You're not easily pushed around, she told us. You're smart and stubborn. A realist."

"Oh." *Way to make me sound deathly boring, Grams,* I thought. *Thanks a lot.*

"So, you want the opposite of her life—you want to be *normal*—so I revised my expectations," he went on. "You'd be studious and serious, I thought, a stickler for the rules and set on your path to the white picket fence and a Volvo in the driveway. You'd study to be a schoolteacher, perhaps, or an accountant." He paused and looked at me with a tilt to his head and a speculative twist to his mouth. "But you dislike school and its restrictions, and you agreed to be friends with me even though I'm...different." His eyes traveled over my face. "You're not what I expected," he said again.

"I'm nothing special," I replied, rubbing my arms against the bumps that had sprung up at his words.

"I disagree," he murmured.

My cheeks flushed again, and I could think of nothing to say, so I was disproportionately grateful to be saved by the arrival of Mr. Gersen.

"All right, everyone. Settle down."

Our burly history teacher always began his classes the same way, taking no notice of whether his students were rowdy enough to warrant the warning. I opened my textbook and tried to concentrate on the lecture. Beside me, Seth listened but took no notes. He said nothing more, but the silence felt loaded. It was the longest class I'd ever had to sit through, and I was still disappointed when the bell rang.

I didn't need to be.

Seth stood when I did, and then followed me out of the room. I turned in the direction of my economics classroom, and he did the same. I wasn't stupid enough to question him and risk ruining the moment, so I kept on as though his company was nothing out of the ordinary.

It was a great plan, until the crowds shifted and there was Finn, walking toward us. There was no way to avoid crossing his path and no way to pretend Seth and I weren't together. I instantly regretted lying to Finn about agreeing to be friends with Seth.

This was what I got for keeping secrets.

"Riley," Finn said, stopping in front of me. His voice was

cool, and his arms were crossed, and my heart sank.

"Finn!" I said brightly, smiling as though I hadn't heard the reproach in his tone. "Have you met Seth yet?"

Finn stuck out his hand, but his expression remained hard. "I'm Finn, Riley's best friend."

Seth took his hand, and that amused smile played on his mouth again. "Seth Callaghan."

"Seth and I are in Mr. Gersen's history class together," I explained.

"Lucky you," Finn replied.

"Finn!" Lizzie shouted as she skipped over to us, her face bright with excitement. She didn't acknowledge me, of course, and gave Seth a quick eyeball before pointedly dismissing him, too.

I'd never been so happy to be interrupted by Lizzie Porter, or anyone else for that matter. I gave her my full attention and prayed the tension around me would dissipate now that Finn was distracted.

"Hi, Lizzie," Finn replied, his voice unnaturally even. "What's up?"

"I'm having a party!" She thrust a pastel pink invitation into his hand. "A big blowout to celebrate our last year of high school. It's going to be wild. You'll be there, right? It's next Friday night."

Finn smiled half-heartedly and gave the pretty paper a cursory glance. "Sure, Lizzie. Sounds great."

"You're invited, too," Lizzie said begrudgingly, barely

meeting my eyes as she handed me an invitation. "And Seth."

"Gee, thanks, Lizzie," I replied, trying my best to dial down the sarcasm.

"We're going to be late for our next class," Seth murmured.

He was right, but I didn't want to agree with him in front of Finn.

"Finn, we have class, too. I'll walk with you?" Lizzie shot me a look with the subtext of victory in it. I wouldn't have been surprised had she poked out her tongue.

"It was nice talking to you," Seth said to Finn.

"Sure, it was," Finn replied.

Finn didn't look at me again before he walked away, Lizzie close at his side. I watched them go, hoping he'd turn and give me a smile or a wave, but he didn't.

"Shall we?" Seth asked.

I turned to look up at him and found his face closer than I was expecting. His lopsided smile jolted my nervous system and I had to focus for a moment on staying upright.

Seth gestured for me to lead, but then lengthened his step to keep up, and as we walked, I noticed he smelled like lavender soap and cold, clean saltwater, fresh and delicious. The fragrance had an oddly soothing effect, and after another two or three inhalations, the muscles in my body relaxed.

I couldn't fix things with Finn until after school. He'd be waiting to walk me home, as we'd agreed—I was certain of that—so for now, I'd let myself enjoy being close to Seth. It felt surreal and temporary, and I was certain it couldn't last.

“This is me,” I said at the door to my economics class, trying hard to remember the next history lesson on my timetable—when I’d get to spend time with Seth again.

“Me too,” he replied, and I was irrationally overjoyed that I could now rely on two classes for my fix of Seth Callaghan.

He followed me in and, this time, I took a seat first.

I intentionally chose the only empty desk in the room, but he didn’t join me straightaway, instead standing over me and waiting with patient eyes as I self-consciously settled myself.

“May I sit here?” he asked finally.

The cynical, often scathing voice in my head—the one I relied on to provide enough entertaining commentary to make school bearable—observed that his manners were a little overdone, yet the judgment had none of its usual rancor. Seth’s formality felt too genuine to deserve it.

“Of course,” I murmured, as he had done for me.

We didn’t speak again, and again he took no notes. I wondered if I was imagining the feel of his eyes on me, because on the few occasions I snuck my own glances in his direction, he was always focused on the teacher, or his textbook, or the view outside the window. After the fourth such disappointment, I resolutely kept my eyes on my work.

When the bell rang to mark the end of the school day, I took my time collecting my things, not wanting the hour to end. As I’d hoped, Seth waited for me, and we were the last to leave the room. He stopped outside the door, and I paused with him, wishing I had a reason to keep him there.

Instead, I stood beside him in silence. This close, I couldn't help meeting his eyes—and once I'd done that, it was impossible to look away. They were deep pools of liquid night, as dark as midnight, and I wanted more of them. I'm not sure how long I stood there, staring.

"I'll see you tomorrow," he said quietly.

It wasn't a question, but I nodded my answer. In truth, I felt a little disconnected from my body, lost in the study of his eyes.

"Bye, Seth," I whispered absently.

With that, he turned and walked away, and he was far down the corridor before I had collected myself. Finally, the purr in my body faded, leaving behind a heartbeat that hitched just a little, and my mind cleared enough that I thought to check my watch. It was fifteen minutes past three, and Finn would be waiting. I spun around and headed in the opposite direction of Seth, my thoughts racing ahead of me as my mind conjured up images of the looming confrontation.

Finn paced impatiently on the edge of the open fields. As soon as I spotted him, I started walking a little faster. I hoped he'd take the flush in my cheeks as evidence of my brisk pace and not the thrill of my time with Seth.

"What are you thinking, Rae?" he demanded the second I was close enough to hear him.

I didn't have to ask what he meant. "He asked me to be friends," I confessed, as if that explained everything.

Finn shook his head. "It's not a good idea. The plan was to stay out of his way, remember?"

"*He* came to *me*. What was I supposed to do?"

"Ah, say no?" he retorted incredulously.

I stared at him blankly, for once at a loss for what to say. Finn threw up his hands, and then started walking toward the trees. I rushed to keep up, and he ran his fingers through his wavy hair, the way he always did when he was thinking about a problem.

"Riley, I don't like him," Finn said eventually, his tone measured. "I don't make a habit of hating people, but I can't help it. His family made my blood curdle."

"I didn't like them much either, but Seth is different."

"How do you figure that?"

"I'm not sure yet. It's just a…feeling," I said sheepishly.

He eyed me askance and I grimaced. We didn't say things like that, me and Finn. They sounded too much like the drivel our families liked to spout.

He stopped suddenly and rounded on me, and I had to pull up short to avoid crashing into him.

"What if I asked you not to talk to him ever again? Would you do that—for me?"

I hesitated, but there was only one answer I could give him. "No, not without a very good reason."

"What if *I* had a feeling, a really bad one?"

"Finn, come on."

"Do you *like* him?"

"I've only just met him!"

Heat burned to my hairline, and I knew I'd given myself away.

Finn's face dropped, his agitation replaced with an emotion I couldn't immediately put a name to. Disappointment, perhaps. I'd let him down.

"Forget it," he snapped, walking away from me again.

I quickly followed and when Finn spoke again, it was with less conviction.

"I'm not happy about this."

I leaped onto his indecision. "You're going to have to trust me," I insisted.

"I do," he murmured, so low I could barely hear him. "It's him I don't trust."

We trekked through the bush to my house, and neither of us mentioned Seth or his family again, but I thought about him the entire way home. I'd hurt my best friend in the whole world for the chance to spend more time with someone I barely knew, and I suddenly realized there was every chance Seth would make me look like a fool.

Dreamer's Log: Agnes (daughter of Brigid)
Day Nineteen of February, Year 1696

Mother died today.

I sat with her and gave my oath I would not tamper with the wards that protect the magic, and I will not—until or unless I believe it necessary. The devil moves closer, I know he does, and I must be ready.

Last night he set an incubus against me, thinking perhaps to test my strength or my resolve before launching an attack of his own. The beautiful, horrible vampire of dreams stalked me day and night for months, tickling my senses in a way that was both discomfiting and enticing. I found the experience interesting.

Mother always begged me to hold my power tight against my skin, but yesterday I'd had enough of the games the incubus plays. I flung my gift out into the world, letting the fire in my body burn brightly as it deserves! Why should I hide it as though it were a source of shame? I let go of every limitation I've ever imposed upon myself, every way I've ever made myself small, and the incubus was unable to turn away from my glory. I drew him to me, like the beguiling flame draws the curious moth—and when he took my dream, I burned him out of existence.

I do not want to believe Mother was disappointed in me when she died. I hope she went to heaven comforted by the knowledge I am stronger and smarter than she ever was, and very capable of killing the monster that waits in the shadows.

CHAPTER SIX

It took all the willpower I had, but I waited until the morning of Lizzie's party to ask Seth if he planned to go.

We'd sat beside each other many times over the last two weeks, but I still found it easier to keep my thoughts straight when I avoided Seth's ebony eyes. I'd lost myself in them more than once. The benefit of these embarrassing slips had been that I'd discovered his eyes, like his hair, were warmer than I'd first thought. The irises were only almost black, somehow made richer and deeper by barely there hints of deep golden brown. Seth seemed mildly entertained by my lapses in concentration.

So, when the bell rang to end our fourth-period history lesson, I kept my eyes on the desk and tried to act casual.

"Are you going to Lizzie's party tonight?" I asked, a little too quickly.

"Are *you* going to Lizzie's party tonight?" he answered.

"I think I am, yes."

"I'm surprised. I didn't think you were interested in traditional social conventions."

"Not many," I admitted, "but I don't mind the occasional party. And it's our final year, after all—it might be fun to celebrate."

Seth looked at me for a long enough time that I started to regret my words. I'd read too much into his interest in me. It was much more likely that his definition of "friends" was exactly that. I rubbed my hands over my arms, trying and failing to soothe the frenetic energy that hummed under my skin whenever I was with him. His eyes moved up and down as he followed the motion of my hands, but he didn't mention what, to him, must have come to look like a weird and persistent habit of mine.

"I don't like to go out at night," he said at last.

It was an odd reason for saying no, too ridiculous for me to believe it.

"Oh, right," I said, wincing at the disappointment in my voice.

"Daylight suits me better," he went on. "Perhaps I could see you over the weekend?"

"Sure," I agreed, certain this was his way of softening the blow of rejection.

His brows drew together as he read my face, and for a moment I thought he might change his mind. Instead, he collected his things and waited to follow me out of the classroom. We sat through our economics class together, but he didn't mention the party again, and I spent the rest of the afternoon feeling lousy about it.

So, I dressed up. I spent most Friday nights with Finn, just the two of us. We'd watch a movie at home or walk down to the beach at dusk and sit on the sand until the stars came out, so my social calendar rarely required that I change out of shorts and T-shirts. Tonight was different. Tonight, I wanted to feel good about myself. I didn't believe I'd be able to forget Seth completely, but I had hope that Lizzie's party would distract me from my despondency for a few hours.

I left my hair down for a change, combing out the tangles until it hung long and straight over my shoulders and down my back. I chose a simple black dress I'd worn only once before—last year for Grams's birthday, when I'd surprised her with a meal at a fancy restaurant. The cut was plain, but it hugged my figure more than any other item of clothing I owned, so I decided it was appropriate for a party. My skin looked paler than usual against the dark fabric, but I decided to embrace it. It worked for Adeline Bennet, didn't it?

Next, I locked myself in the bathroom and pulled out my tiny cosmetics case. I didn't usually wear makeup—it wasn't practical or comfortable, given the almost year-round heat—but I had a few items in my collection, all free samples.

I pulled out a tube of mascara and ran the wet bristles through my eyelashes. Instantly, they looked longer and thicker, my green eyes wider and brighter. Unsure how to apply the pretty pink rouge correctly, I used the little brush to dust a tiny amount over my cheekbones. I finished with lipstick that I applied carefully inside my lip line, but when

I was done, I had second thoughts. It looked redder than I'd anticipated so I checked the label: *Bloodlust*. Unhappy with the shade, I used a square of tissue to blot away most of it but, even then, my lips appeared plumper than they really were.

Resigned to the fact that, with my limited beauty knowledge, I couldn't do any better than I'd already done, I dragged my hair to the side so I could inspect the jewelry on my ears. Then, I did something I'd never done before. I removed my earrings—all of them, except the clovers. I picked up the silver trinket box I'd brought with me from my bedroom, where I kept it hidden underneath the clothes in my dresser, and opened the lid. I used my finger to move the contents around and selected five new earrings, all made from plated gold and sparkling colored glass and, possibly, a few real gems, but I couldn't be sure.

Over the years I'd amassed a small collection of earrings, given as gifts, or bought on a whim when I'd fallen in love with them walking past a shop window. I'd never worn any of them because Grams insisted I wear only silver. I'd never challenged her on it because it meant more to her than it did to me, but I'd promised myself that, one day, I'd wear my secret earrings when the occasion was right. Tonight, I decided, was the night.

I dropped my silver earrings into the box and closed the lid. Looking at my reflection one last time, I arranged my hair over my shoulders again, hiding my ears from view. I wanted to enjoy myself tonight, not start the evening with an argument. What Grams didn't know wouldn't hurt her.

Right on time, Finn knocked on the front door. I ducked into my room to stash my earrings and slip on my sandals, then ran down the stairs.

"Riley!" Grams exclaimed.

I froze at the surprise in her voice and then rolled my eyes, looking to Finn for moral support, but the shock on his face was just as bad.

"Seriously, you two, it's only a dress," I said, but I tugged at the hem a little. Was it too short?

"Of course, it is. Don't mind me." Grams waved her hands to indicate the space next to Finn. "Stand there. Let me take a picture."

As I did as I was told, I realized I wasn't the only one who had gone to a little extra effort tonight. Finn wore a light-blue collared shirt that clung to his chest and arms, and dark jeans I'd never seen before. I stood next to him and he put an arm around my waist. He smelled like cologne and I was unusually aware of the way my hip brushed against his leg, how his hand hovered against my lower back, not quite touching the fabric of my dress.

The coy look Grams gave us didn't help matters.

"There," she said, having snapped us with her ancient camera. "You two look wonderful together."

"Goodnight, Grams," I said pointedly, taking the camera from her hands and giving her an exasperated look. "I'll be home about midnight."

"I'll be in bed by then," she smiled, amused by my embarrassment. "Lock the door behind you when you get in."

Finn opened the front door for me and did the same when we reached his car. He didn't say a word until he'd reversed down the driveway.

"Are we excited?" he asked, grinning widely.

"Sure, can't you tell?"

I tried to feign indifference, but the truth was, I was a little pumped.

"You're all about the happy dance," he laughed.

Finn's enthusiasm was infectious. He turned up the radio and drummed his hands against the steering wheel in time with the music, and I sang along whenever I recognized the lyrics. We cruised onto Lizzie's street about ten minutes later, and the party had well and truly started. She'd decorated her front yard with twinkling lights, and music blared from a sound system.

"Finn, you made it!"

Lizzie bounced over to the car and opened the driver's side door as soon as Finn cut the engine. Her long hair was woven into loose braids, her skin was smooth and suntanned—and she had a lot of it on show. Her tight fluorescent-yellow dress displayed her flat midriff and long legs, and I felt a flash of inadequacy as I stepped out of the car.

"Hey, Lizzie," Finn greeted her.

"Can I get you a drink?" she asked.

"Sure. Rae, you ready?"

I joined him on the other side of the car. The night air was warm, and I lifted my hair off my neck to cool myself down. I was reconsidering my decision to wear it loose, regretting the elastic band I'd left on the bathroom vanity. Perhaps Lizzie would part with one for a few hours. I'd have to ask her.

"Rae, what happened to your earrings?"

Finn reached over to touch the metal decorating my ears. He moved in closer, and his fingers were warm as they brushed my jaw, my neck, my ear. My skin pebbled, and I sucked in a breath as my body responded to his touch.

"I changed them," I whispered.

"Looks good," he murmured, meeting my eyes and smiling crookedly, as though he knew the effect he was having on me.

I shoved against his chest, annoyance and embarrassment flushing my skin with heat. "Get lost, Finn."

"What did I do?"

I stalked into the party, bypassing the front door and heading straight to Lizzie's backyard via the side gate. The music was louder there, and people were pressed together on a temporary dance floor marked out beside the speakers on the deck. In the far corner of the yard, Lizzie's in-ground pool was filled with swimmers, their screams and splashes adding to the decibel count. A small firepit crackled and smoked in the opposite corner, filling the air with the smells of campgrounds and burnt marshmallows. It was loud but not unpleasant, so I grabbed a bottle of lemonade from an icy bucket hidden under a table loaded with food and found a seat to the side where I could people-watch.

It took Finn only a few minutes to find me. He stood awkwardly for a minute.

"Do you want to swim?" he asked finally.

"I didn't bring my swimmers," I replied shortly.

"Do you want to dance?"

"Maybe later."

Lizzie popped up out of nowhere. "I'll dance with you, Finn."

Finn hesitated but, when I said nothing, he let Lizzie drag him away. I leaned back in my chair, feeling disappointed that my good mood had soured so quickly, and a little confused about why. I didn't know if I was mad at Finn or myself, so I sat there, alone and at a loss for what to do next.

I finished my lemonade and watched the party guests flit between the pool and the dance floor. Forty-five minutes later, Finn hadn't returned, and I decided I'd had enough fun for one night.

Jonas Vella lingered nearby, scoping out the snacks, so I stood and joined him.

"I'm leaving now," I said. "If you see Finn, can you let him know I decided to walk home?"

"No problem," Jonas replied distractedly. I had little confidence he'd remember to pass on my message, but then I decided that it didn't matter. Finn would know I'd left when—if—he came looking for me again.

It wasn't a long walk home and the night was mild, so I didn't mind. I started down the driveway and left Lizzie's house, with its bright lights and frenetic noise and maddening best friend, behind me.

Dreamer's Log: Agnes (daughter of Brigid)
Day One of May, Year 1712

My daughter, Lucy, would have been a bright dreamer, but Lucy died today.

She leaves me her daughter, Cecilia.

CHAPTER SEVEN

I welcomed the silence of the dark, open street because, in the stillness, I could think clearly again. I realized that not only was I disappointed that, despite what he'd said, Seth hadn't surprised me at Lizzie's party, I was also starting to resent Finn's teasing. We'd always had that kind of relationship, neither of us taking anything too seriously, but lately, the good-natured taunts about his non-existent attraction to me felt a little too…personal.

And now, it was obvious I also had a thing for Seth—who I'd all but asked out, and who had all but turned me down.

I groaned quietly as an annoying comparison occurred to me. I was a million times more pathetic than Lizzie Porter could ever be.

After too long in my head, my thoughts crashing around in frustration and confusion, I looked up to get my bearings and stopped short when I realized I'd overshot the corner of my street. Here, on the edge of town, the houses were few and far between, and all set back from the road, so it was dark and quiet. I must have been walking while distracted for a good five minutes.

Turning to retrace my steps, I froze when my eyes snagged on a shadowy figure standing still in the middle of the road. It didn't move, which alarmed me. Anyone going about their business wouldn't have paused to stare at me in the dark. My mouth dried and my stomach clenched. I forced my feet to take one step, and then another, but they wouldn't cooperate more than that.

"Hello," the figure said in a deep, smooth voice.

It reminded me of Seth's voice, or Perry's, so sweet and soothing, like a lullaby, and I forgot all about running. I stood and stared into the shadows, desperate to see the figure's face.

"That's better," my stranger crooned.

He started toward me, but he wasn't moving fast enough. I wanted him near me now. I stepped forward as he did, and we met in a pool of streetlight.

His face, so lovely, stopped the breath in my throat. I didn't know him, but he was familiar. His skin was flawlessly smooth and so pale, almost incandescent. Black eyes burned brightly out of a magnificent face, all even planes and perfect proportions. He smiled, his soft lips parting slowly to reveal straight white teeth that gleamed wetly in the dull light.

He placed a cold hand on my neck, and I trembled at his touch. My stranger smiled down at me as he shifted his hand to cup my head and tilt it ever so slightly. I leaned into him, contentedly pressing my cheek against the palm of his hand.

The sizzle of burning flesh sounded in my ear, and my

beautiful stranger jerked back, hissing and holding his hand to his chest as though injured.

I felt ashamed. I'd done something wrong.

A streak of darkness shot through the night, solidifying into a man as it connected with my stranger. The impact drove both bodies too far down the road, neither of them touching the ground until they collided with the asphalt, sounding almost like a car wreck. I shrank back from the noise but couldn't tear my eyes away.

With movements too fast to follow, the figures exchanged blows. It was a ballet of violence, each move quick and precise, each countermove quicker and more vicious than the last. I watched as the man fell and recovered, then fell again, and then finally gained an advantage by pinning my stranger to the ground with a knee pushed into his back. He set his hands around my stranger's head and started to twist, then stopped. He looked up at me and my heart pounded.

"Riley," he breathed.

His angel's voice sang to me, soft and urgent. I stepped toward it.

"No, Riley. Turn around. Go home."

I wanted to do as he said. I didn't want to leave him. My body thrummed.

"No," I whispered, shaking my head.

The man sighed, exasperated. Angels weren't supposed to feel impatience. "Riley. Go home. Go to your room. Change your earrings. Go to bed."

It was harder this time to deny him, but the desire to be near him was stronger than the compulsion to do as he said.

"No."

His laugh was self-deprecating. Musical. I stepped forward again. My stranger, prostrate on the ground, growled and struggled to free himself. His captor shifted his knee, pressing into my stranger's spine, eliciting a crunch like crushing stone.

The angelic man looked at me thoughtfully and cocked his head. "What if I promise to meet you there?" he asked reluctantly.

I contemplated his offer, my rational self at war with my ongoing befuddlement. This seemed an acceptable compromise.

I was three steps in the opposite direction before I realized I'd obeyed him. I spun around to object again, but the man was gone and with him, my stranger. The road was empty but for me.

I shuddered as the silence and solitude cleared the fog from my mind. I looked around into the night, feeling alone and vulnerable, and then I did what any sensible person in my position would do.

I ran.

I sprinted down the road, gratefully turning the corner onto my street. My legs pumped painfully as I tried to outpace my thoughts, but they nipped at my heels the entire way home.

I'd been approached by a man who looked and spoke and moved in a way that reminded me of Grams's new friends.

He had been different the way they had been different, yet it had been more than that. His energy had been more palpable. He was fast, and strong, and more powerful than I could comprehend—than any human could comprehend.

And there was the thought I wanted to leave behind. The stranger couldn't have been human at all. Knowing that was impossible didn't make it any less true, and while a tiny voice in my head screamed at me to slow down and really *think* about what that meant, a larger part of me refused.

All I could accept at that moment was the stranger had meant to harm me. I'd been in serious trouble, no doubt about it.

And Seth Callaghan had saved me.

So, I ran. I ran toward the safety behind the walls of my house but, more than that, I ran toward the promise of Seth.

I'd forgotten all about Lizzie's party and my fight with Finn until I was close enough to my front yard to see his car parked in the driveway. He was leaning against the driver's side hood, his phone in his hand and his attention all on my front door, so he didn't see me approach.

"Finn?" I asked between gasps for breath.

"Riley!" he exhaled, sagging with relief. "Where have you been? Why didn't you answer your phone?"

My phone was in my hand, and I lifted it to check the screen. Finn had called me four times and sent twice as many texts. I hadn't registered the vibrations in my hand. I'd been too distracted.

"I didn't hear it," I replied lamely.

His eyes narrowed, taking in my heaving chest. "Something happened."

I hesitated. "There was a guy…"

Finn's face hardened, and he pushed away from the car.

"Are you okay?" he asked.

"I'm fine. I ran home."

"Who was it? Where is he?" Finn looked out into the darkness behind me, searching.

"I don't know. I didn't recognize him."

Finn stared at me, wanting more than my vague explanation, which sounded thin even to my ears.

"Nothing happened," I added. "There was a guy walking down the street. It was dark and he gave me the creeps, so I ran."

Finn shook his head and sagged, dropping his eyes and leaning back on the car again. "You didn't answer your phone, and I didn't want to wake Grams and worry her."

"It's not your fault. I'm okay."

"That's something, at least." It was his turn to hesitate. "Do you want to hang out a little longer? It's not midnight yet, so you haven't broken curfew. I'll stay a while, just until you're not so shaken up."

It took all my strength to meet his eyes as I said, "Not tonight. I'm too tired."

"You don't look tired," he disagreed. "You're pretty keyed up, Rae."

"I'm fine, really," I assured him, forcing my breath to slow and my legs to stop shaking. I smiled in a way I hoped would reassure him. "I'll see you tomorrow, okay?"

He contemplated me in silence for too long, and I worried that he'd insist on keeping me company. Any other time, I'd have agreed to watch a movie or make him a late-night snack but tonight, I wanted Finn to leave.

"If that's what you want," he said at last, shrugging unhappily, and my smile faltered under a hot wave of guilt.

I waited outside to be sure his car had cleared the driveway before I opened my front door. I felt sick about keeping a secret from Finn, but the nausea was easy to ignore. I was too impatient to see Seth again, to be near him and hear his voice, to know he was safe, and to ask him exactly what it was that had happened tonight.

Dreamer's Log: Agnes (daughter of Brigid)
Day Thirty-One of July, Year 1732

Cecilia was destined to be an even brighter dreamer than her mother, but Cecilia died today.

She leaves me her daughter, Edith.

CHAPTER EIGHT

The house inside was dark but for the glow of a lamp Grams had left on in the living room. I tiptoed upstairs and opened Grams's bedroom door just enough to peek in and check she was sleeping soundly. The hinges squeaked a little and my heart lurched, but she didn't stir.

I slowly closed the door, and then crept to my room at the other end of the hall. It was dark, so I shut the door and switched on my bedside light. I changed into clothes that were more comfortable, and then slipped silently into the bathroom to scrub the cosmetics from my face and brush my teeth. Finally, I changed my earrings. I didn't understand why Seth had asked me to do it but, considering he'd just saved me from a highly dangerous situation, I decided to worry about the why of it later.

With the silver in my ears and my hair again pulled up into its usual knot, I returned to the front door. For a moment I fancied that I could sense Seth on the other side, that the ripples under my skin were a psychic response to his presence.

I opened it and, as I'd hoped, he was waiting for me. My heart sped up at the sight of him standing so still and so perfect, right there on my dilapidated porch.

"Hello, Riley," he said.

I was again taken by his height. Only this close to him was I so aware that he stood head and shoulders over me. Tonight, he had the sleeves of his dark gray shirt rolled up to display his pale, sculpted forearms, and the button at the collar open to expose the hollow at his throat. His small smile was hesitant, no longer confident, but his face was no less captivating. On the contrary, his uncertainty made him more attractive.

"Hello," I said, surprised at the tremor in my voice. The adrenaline was starting to dissipate, leaving behind raw nerves and an almost unbearable sense of overwhelm that had nothing to do with what had already happened tonight, and everything to do with what still might come.

"Would you like to talk?" he asked, his eyebrows drawn and his tone underscored with concern.

I nodded, not trusting myself to speak. He made no move to come in, instead turning to sit on the love seat Grams kept on the porch. I joined him, rocking the chair a little as I lowered myself into it. As it eased to stillness, the silence grew. Seth waited for me to break it.

"What happened tonight?" I whispered.

"What do *you* think happened?"

I wasn't anticipating his question, and so I didn't have a coherent answer prepared.

"There was a man—or perhaps *not* a man—standing in the middle of the road, and he was terrifying, and beautiful. I was scared, but I wanted to go to him. And his hand was so cold. Then you appeared, and…you saved me."

I scrubbed my face as tears spilled onto my cheeks.

"I'm sorry, Riley," he said gently. "You were in danger. I had no choice but to do as I did."

I shook my head impatiently. Seth had misunderstood my point. "But who was he? *What* was he?"

What are you? I amended silently.

"Riley, what do you know about Maggie's superstitions?"

The way he said Grams's name rang with familiarity. It sharpened my wits—and my tone. "What do you mean?"

"I realize you do not believe as she does but you should understand the theory, at the very least. Can you tell me what you know?"

"It's going to sound ridiculous," I warned him.

He smiled his amused smile. "Try me," he replied.

I met his onyx eyes and registered their black depths with new insight. My blood chilled, and the words came out as though dragged.

"She thinks the truths of our destinies are hidden inside our dreams. She says there are demons in the world who hunt humans in the night, and only silver can protect us, body and soul, from the evil that stalks us by moonlight."

"And what more do you know about these demons?" he pressed.

When I was young enough to listen with rapture to her stories, Grams would read to me from her books every night without exception. As I grew older, her stories became less entertaining and I stopped regarding them with childlike wonder. When I finally understood that Grams actually believed her tales to be true, I refused to listen anymore simply on principle—and I'd had my ears stopped up tight to them ever since.

Yet, despite my resistance, enough of her words had stuck in those early years. Now, a certain passage surfaced from my memory. Involuntarily, I recited it by rote, word-perfect without pause.

"'And the sons and the daughters of the Master of Fear were beautiful, desirable demons, with eyes that were black with the thirst for our blood and their own veins a-boil with their desire for pain.'"

Seth's face was impassive as he watched my mind tick over.

"Vampires?" I whispered.

He stood so quickly, he appeared not to move at all—first he was in one place, and then another. My heart thumped painfully.

Uncertainty still marked his lovely face. "Would you like me to leave?"

I shook my head mechanically. "No."

He didn't return to the space next to me on the love seat, but instead took two steps further away before picking up our conversation.

"I don't know where to start," he admitted with a frown.

"Who was the man in the road?" I whispered.

He appeared glad for the prompt, nodding and visibly collecting himself. "A vampire," Seth confirmed and, although I already knew the answer, hearing it from his lips was a finger of icy fear tracing the line of my spine. "The traditional sort, you might call him," Seth continued. "One of those demons Maggie warned you about, the kind who stalks humans in the night."

"To drink our blood?" I added tentatively.

Seth watched for my reaction as he replied. "Yes, to drink your blood."

I couldn't hide the shudder that rippled through my body.

"He looked like you, pale and beautiful." I blushed and dropped my eyes as I heard my own words, then rushed on to cover my embarrassment. "He was strong and fast, and so were you. His hand was so cold—" Another hand, as frigid as the one I remembered, gently lifted my chin. I met Seth's gaze and shivered again. "—like yours."

He held my eyes as though searching them for his own answers.

"Are you…?" I couldn't finish the question, but Seth understood.

"A vampire?"

I nodded and waited for him to confirm what I already knew.

"I am," he said.

I gave myself a moment to absorb his confession, but Seth must have misunderstood the silence because he volunteered more detail without my asking for it.

"I say your assailant was the traditional sort because while he, and those like him, would have murdered you without hesitation, there are a handful of others, like my family and myself, who are more…alternative. We survive almost entirely on animal blood and on the uncommon occasions we do feed on humans, we do not kill them nor take pleasure in causing them pain."

"Grams has always made a point of telling me that demons are deranged with thirst," I reasoned out loud. "They are the enemy, and yet here you are—"

"I want your blood," Seth interrupted, his eyes burning excitedly for a very quick second before his face was still again. "It calls to me this very minute, but I've had a lot of practice denying that particular craving. I can resist."

"Oh." There seemed no correct way to respond to his unexpected declaration.

"Are you afraid?"

I considered him and wondered how much of the truth I should share. I'd already admitted I thought him beautiful, what would another disclosure matter now?

"Honestly? I'm terrified," I admitted with a nervous chuckle.

He took a quick step back, and his expression faded into a dull blankness. "I'll go."

"But you saved me," I added hastily, and my words tumbled over each other as I rushed to get them out before my nerves—or Seth, either one—deserted me. "And I like you. I'm…confused."

I expected him to laugh, or at the least tease me gently to mask the discomfort of having to reject me, but he said nothing, only stared quietly, and heat rushed to my face again.

"I like you, too, Riley," he finally replied.

Seth studied me as the silence hung heavy in the air. I could think of nothing worthwhile to say to break it, and so I stared at my hands.

"I do have one small problem," he said abruptly, returning to sit by me on the love seat, closer this time, though still not near enough to touch me. "You weren't supposed to find out about me. Not now, at least, and most certainly not like this."

I'd missed something here. My brain screamed at me to keep up, and then I was thinking out loud.

"Your father is a vampire, and he was here last week, visiting my Grams," I said.

"Yes," he said simply.

"Grams never thought you were just fellow believers, interested in her stories," I accused. "She knows you're vampires. She's always known."

It wasn't a question, because I was certain I had it right, but Seth validated my words anyway.

"Yes."

I slumped into the seat and closed my eyes to better sort my thoughts. If Grams was right about vampires—and I was floating outside of my body by even allowing that idea residency in my head—she'd made an unthinkable concession for Perry and his family by inviting them into our home. And even more distressing was, why had she let me deny and defy her all these years? With *friends* like Perry, Grams could have shown me the proof long ago.

"Her superstitions are more than that," Seth went on. His voice sounded clearer and more musical with my eyes shut. "They form the foundations of vampire canon, almost all of them true. Silver, for example."

I touched my earrings, and a detail of the night's events resolved in my memory.

"My earring burned that vampire's hand," I murmured.

"It did," Seth agreed. "Never remove these, Riley. Promise me that. Silver charms will encourage a stalking vampire to look elsewhere for prey, and while you wear it at your ears, silver can keep your dreams safe while you sleep."

"Do they bother you?" I asked, curious.

He smiled wryly. "They aren't pleasant, but I do not intend to touch them. Now to return to my first problem. I've messed up by allowing you to witness my natural behaviors—the strength, the speed—and I need to ask you a favor."

"Anything," I agreed quickly.

His smile widened, and I chastised myself for giving away so much.

"Could you go on for a while longer behaving as though nothing has changed? Maggie has extracted oaths from us all that we will not risk her secrets until she says the time is right. My understanding is she intends to share the details with you once you turn eighteen, and that's only a few months away. Could you say nothing until then?"

I thought about what Seth was asking me, and while my desperate impulse in that moment was to agree to anything he requested, I retained enough clarity and determination to ask for one last answer before we settled on anything.

"Who else knows about you, Seth?"

"Harry, and his family," Seth responded willingly.

"Finn?" My stomach twisted. "Does he know what you are?"

"He does."

"He never told me." My voice sounded strangled.

"He wasn't supposed to."

My eyes stung and my head spun dizzily so I rested it between my hands. Everyone I loved—everyone who was supposed to love me—had been lying to me about something incredible.

"Can you do it?" Seth asked. "Can you pretend to not know the truth?"

Like a flipped switch, white-hot rage burned through my blood, and I pushed away all doubt. I was a terrible liar and I'd never kept a secret from Finn—I'd rarely had reason to be dishonest with Grams, for that matter—yet at that moment, the idea of withholding important information from them seemed like a brilliant idea.

"I can," I promised.

Seth stood again. "I should go." He looked into the darkness as though someone waited for him there.

I got to my feet and stood as close to him as I dared. "Will you come back?"

He looked at me gravely and, for a moment, I was certain he would tell me no. Instead, he said, "Maggie would suspect something was wrong if we spent too much time together." He paused, and then continued carefully. "And Finn would not like it."

"They don't need to know," I argued.

"And how would we keep it from them?" His tone was amused.

I shrugged deliberately, to convey how simple it could be, to assure him how little I worried about these things. "Visit me after Grams is asleep."

"I can't sit on your front porch every night," he said. "And nighttime isn't...prudent."

"Just come again tomorrow night, please? Around midnight. We can discuss the details then."

He paused, and as I searched for ways I might convince him, he finally said, "I will." My heart fluttered fitfully and I was already feeling the ecstatic tension of anticipation when he added, "But I wager that once I've answered more of your questions, you won't be so ready to invite me back again."

Dreamer's Log: Edith (daughter of Cecilia)
Day Fifteen of November, Year 1751

The dream is still so mysterious to me, and I find it incredibly frustrating that Grandmother Agnes is of such fragile mind.

No, not frustrating. Terrifying.

Her ill health becomes more apparent each day. When we walk together in the dream, I try not to press her too often on the whereabouts of the magic, but as time goes on, fear compels me to ask my questions more frequently. Alas, any suggestion that we seek out the magic, to reset its wards and ensure its safety, is met with resistance bordering on aggression—much like her temperament in the waking world.

And so, I fear she has forgotten the way.

I have scoured every book, read every word she has written, but Grandmother Agnes's journals have grown lean in recent years, and never has she put on paper the path to the magic. She was never supposed to. That is not our way.

We are meant to learn these secrets in the laps and dreams of our mothers.

I do not know what will become of us—me, my daughter, our friends who hunt vampires on Earth, even humanity itself—should my great-grandmother pass without recalling where she hid the magic, without sharing with me the spells she uses to protect it from evil.

I greatly fear the devil will find it first, and all will be lost.

No. I will not allow that to pass while the watch is mine. I have read in Grandmother Margaret's and Grandmother Kateryn's logs of other ways to walk the dream, ways that dear Agnes has either entirely forgotten or chooses to withhold from me, and I have started to read fortunes. It may all be nonsense and I dare not speak it out loud, even to Grandmother Agnes, for the words on my lips make me feel a charlatan.

Nevertheless, for the sake of my daughter, and for hers after that, I believe I may have divined a way to find light among the shadows.

CHAPTER NINE

I slept fitfully that night. I was too wired to rest so it was nearly three a.m. by the time I was weary enough to turn out the lights. Again, although I never usually dreamed, I was tormented by almost-pictures and half-formed visions that flickered like static behind my eyelids. There was no color in them, only varied shades of gray and flashes of light that startled me out of sleep over and over. Aside from exhausted, the pictures also made me feel uneasy, but I decided that should be expected, given the evening I'd just had. I eventually passed out in the early hours of the morning and slept through until noon.

When I woke, groggy and dazed, it took me a few moments to remember everything that had happened. It was only seconds later that my memories returned and, when they did, I lay still and replayed everything that happened.

The party. The attack. My rescue.

Seth.

I ran through the details more times than was necessary, then, when I tired of that, I moved on to listing ways I could fill what remained of the day. My end point was midnight, when I would be with Seth again. The in-between, usually spent with Grams and Finn, was decidedly unappealing today.

There was only one thing to do. Avoid it altogether.

I picked up my phone. The screen was lit up with two texts from Finn, both sent earlier that morning. Each one was a question about my plans for the day.

I should have felt bad about lying to him, but I was too angry. I typed out a short message, telling him I had a headache and wanted to sleep. Hoping that would be the end of it, my stomach twisted when he replied almost immediately to tell me he hoped I felt better soon. I squashed down the guilt and reminded myself he'd been lying to me for five years about things much more important than a headache.

There was a light tap on my door, and it opened slowly to reveal Grams's stooped figure. When she saw I was awake, she smiled and moved all the way into my room. I tried to ignore the hurt and the rage and the confusion I felt when I looked at my great-grandmother, the woman who raised me, but I'd never had a good poker face, so I rolled over and buried my head in my pillow.

Her smooth, cool hand brushed the hair back from my face as she tried to feel my skin for heat. I shrugged her away, not wanting to be touched.

"What's the matter, Riley?" she asked, worry tightening her voice. "You've slept all day. Do you feel unwell?"

"It's only a headache," I mumbled, the words muffled by

the pillow. I turned my head just enough to speak clearly. "I didn't sleep very well last night."

"Why didn't you sleep well?" Grams asked sharply. "Did you dream?"

I groaned in annoyance. "No, Grams. You know I don't dream. It was a long night, and I'm still a little tired."

She didn't reply, only shuffled out of my room. I heard her opening cupboards in the kitchen, then turning on the faucet. When she returned, she handed me two aspirin and a large glass of water.

"This will help," she said, handing over the pills first. I took them and dropped them into my mouth, then chased them with a gulp of the water.

"Thanks," I muttered.

"I'm due to go out for my exercise class," Grams said, watching me thoughtfully. "But I can stay, if you'd rather not be alone."

"No," I replied, a little too quickly. I tried again, doing my best to sound unwell. "I mean, I'm just going to go back to sleep and there's no need for you to be here for that."

I attempted a smile that felt false, but Grams seemed to buy it. She nodded and turned toward the door.

"Are you sure about the dreams?" she asked again, pausing with her hand on the doorknob.

I recalled the strange gray shapes and disturbing lights that had interrupted my rest for half the night but dismissed them immediately. I'd never had a real dream before, but

I was certain they were nothing like that. Real dreams were like movies in your mind, made with a rainbow of colors, recalling people and places that made you feel good.

"I'm sure, Grams," I said.

She nodded noncommittally but apparently decided that whatever my ailment, she didn't need to stay. As soon as she'd left my room, I sighed in relief.

I waited until I heard Grams lock the front door behind her before I jumped up to watch her from the window. Her bent little shape made its way down the drive with a level of speed that belied her age. She stopped at the curb and, like clockwork, a shiny red sedan pulled up alongside. The driver—a neighbor named Angela who, at fifty-five years old, was almost thirty years Grams's junior—leaped out, clad in bright pink Lycra tights, and skirted around the hood of the car to help Grams into her seat. Satisfied that the older woman was safely ensconced, Angela returned to her side, slipped in behind the wheel and quickly took off, reaching the speed limit almost instantaneously. When the car had disappeared around the far bend in the road, I let myself breathe.

I knew what I had to do.

I didn't usually spend time in Grams's bedroom. She tidied it herself, washed all her own linens, and rarely found a reason to invite me in. It was also where she kept a library of books and a collection of knickknacks related to her superstitions.

Once upon a time, she'd stored them in the living room

on shelves and tables that she kept meticulously free of dust and fingerprints but, as I grew older—and more obstinately opposed to her strange ways—she'd transferred all the objects and texts she considered precious to her private space. We'd never spoken about it, and it had suited me well enough that I'd never stopped to consider why she'd capitulated to me so easily. I'd never believed she'd done it to keep things from me—after all, she had tried for years to tell me the stories written on those pages—but in light of recent revelations, I had new reasons to be suspicious.

The door to Grams's bedroom was closed, so I opened it and let myself in. The small space was furnished with dark, heavy timber furniture that gleamed dully in the light from the window, where thick drapes in rich green were tied back to let in the afternoon sun. Her beige bedspread was patterned with blush-colored roses, the pink shade on her bedside lamp was finished with tassels, and the three silver-framed photos beneath it were of me, and my mother, and my grandmother.

I picked up those two and stared at the faces smiling back at me. The photos were old and taken in different decades, but the women in them were similar in age—mid-twenties, I estimated. They looked alike, both with long dark hair, smooth ivory skin, wide hazel eyes. My thumb stroked the glass over my mother's cheek.

Grams and I had lost so much, and I wondered if, perhaps, she hadn't told me about Seth—about vampires—

because she wanted to protect me. Maybe she didn't want to lose any more.

I set the pictures down. This was going to be more complicated than I anticipated.

My sudden flash of insight made me feel more cautious, and more forgiving of Grams's reasons for lying to me, but it didn't extinguish my curiosity completely, so I revised my intentions. I would not deliberately search for things Grams wanted to keep hidden. I had no real desire to snoop among her personal belongings. Instead, I would look for information about the things Grams had tried to teach me long ago—information about demons, and vampires.

Information about Seth.

These were the types of things I could find in Grams's books, and they were all there on the small bookshelf under her window. I recognized most of them, the spines facing outward with familiar colors and lettering that reminded me of my childhood.

I fell to the carpeted floor beside the shelves and pulled out the thickest book, an old text on demon mythology that Grams used to flip through with me snuggled up on her lap. I was too young, then, to read the words, but the illustrations were as I remembered: hand-drawn sketches in broad strokes and faded colors. Here, a creature with gnarled yellowed horns showing through a mane of dark coarse hair. There, a traditional-looking devil with red skin and a bare torso. Next, an ordinary-looking man, oddly handsome, staring out of the page with fevered black eyes. He was dressed in plain linens and had a belt of bulky pouches tied around his waist.

I impatiently turned page after page, searching for an image that looked like Seth. Finally, toward the end, I found it. There were two pictures, in fact. A man on the left, and opposite him, a woman.

The man was tall and lean of muscle, extremely pale and dressed in dark, well-fitting clothes. His hair was black and thick, his eyes as dark, and he stood with an arrogant lift to his chin and an amused twist to his lips that reminded me of Seth—just a little. He was angelic in his loveliness.

The woman in the picture could very well have been Adeline: ivory-skinned, slender, painfully beautiful. Dark hair in a loose braid cascaded over one shoulder, her dark eyes smoldered alluringly and she wore a dress that covered her from the neck to the ankle yet hugged her slight figure in all the right places. Her parted lips were plump and pink.

Scrawled under each was a label: *vampire (left—male, right—female).*

My hand shook slightly as I turned the page, and I shifted my jaw a little to work moisture back into my mouth.

There in black and white were two pages of tightly handwritten words describing vampires in expert detail. I scanned them desperately, and when I was done, I sucked in a deep breath and returned to the beginning to read it all again, slowly this time, to be sure I hadn't missed anything.

It was terrifying. It was fascinating.

Of all the creatures created by the Master of Fear, only one did survive to stalk with horror the realm of the living. The others he made were too weak for our world and were banished to hell or the halls of our nightmares. Do not mourn them—rejoice now in their deaths!—but do not raise your grateful eyes to the heavens for long, for the single demon who remains on Earth is the most deadly of all, and he shall come upon you when you least expect it.

Made in the human image of the Master of Fear yet fashioned with a beauty he does not possess, the vampire is pleasing to the eye—more pleasing than any human ever was or could be. The lines of his face will enchant you, the curve of his mouth beguile you, and the perfection of his body seduce you.

Her skin, pale and chill, is as white and as cold as fresh-fallen snow because the vampire owns no blood of her own, has no heat in her veins, hosts no life in her chest. Inside, the vampire is dead.

His existence is infinite and sustained by desire: the craving for blood and the hunger for pain. The immortal vampire will drink lustily of your life and find pleasure in the torment he inflicts in the taking.

She will hold you as a lover and you will beg her for death as you writhe in excruciating pleasure, for that is the power of the vampire.

Beware the vampire.

He runs with unnatural speed. He moves with unnatural strength. He possesses unnatural senses. He hunts with unnatural stealth.

But while you may believe that all hope is lost, these truths make up not the whole of it.

The vampire can be vulnerable once, twice, and thrice.

The vampire hunts in the night when his supernatural skill is at its peak, because in sunlight he is weakened to the point of despair. So diminished is his speed, his strength, his senses, his stealth that a slayer may meet him then on favorable ground. Therefore, if there is one who seeks to kill this demon, approach him at noon under a blazing sun. Only then can you hope for success.

With all his speed and strength, the vampire will evade an enemy, but a slayer can overcome him with weapons of blessed silver. Hot do they burn the cold skin of the vampire and weakened is the vampire burdened with a silver charm. A silver dagger in his heart is the vampire's death, but the brave slayer who wields the deadly blade must burn the body and collect the ashes to be interred in silver, to prevent the vampire rising again.

And for that rarest of vampires—that hybrid demon conceived in error by the Master of Fear, that monster who steals into mortal dreams and makes a playground of the aether within, that abominable one who claims human souls for his own—a fate worse than death awaits. For this vampire and this vampire alone—called the incubus he, and the succubus she—there in the dream awaits a witch of great power, and there she will smite him most certainly and lethally.

For the incubus struck down by the witch of dreams, there is no way back.

My heart was beating too fast. When my head started to spin, I realized I'd stopped breathing. I exhaled gustily, and then deliberately inhaled very slowly in an effort to return my pulse to its regular rhythm. My blood wouldn't cooperate, so I gave up on breathing and started to pace.

Everything I'd read in Grams's book aligned with the characteristics and behaviors I'd observed in Seth: his pale skin and frozen touch, his overwhelming allure and surreal beauty. I didn't think the text did that part justice, but I also couldn't find words of my own to better describe the way Seth looked. Then there was the speed, and the strength, and the aversion to silver.

I recalled things Seth had said to me in the last two weeks, strange comments that had made no sense at the time. The first was his reluctance to meet me at night when, it seemed, he'd be at his strongest and I would be most vulnerable. Another was asking me to always wear my silver earrings, and his confession that he did not intend to touch them.

Seth was trying to protect me.

I was positive Seth was nothing like the vampires described in Grams's old book. Those words had been written hundreds of years ago, during times of medieval superstition and unreasonable fear about things people couldn't understand. Sure, there were bloodthirsty demons out there—one had stalked me in my own neighborhood, after all—but it couldn't be as simple as that, not when there was such a creature as Seth.

What had he called the vampire who attacked me? I wracked my brain as I recalled our conversation from the night before. *The traditional sort,* he had said. It only stood to reason, I decided, that Seth was a modern vampire. Different. Better. *Good.*

I closed Grams's book and returned it to the shelf. Sweeping my glance around the room to be sure I hadn't obviously disturbed anything, I stepped out into the hall and closed the bedroom door behind me. My thoughts skittered as wildly as my racing heart.

Could I have feelings for a *vampire*?

It made no sense. I wasn't so far gone that I didn't know it was absurd. I barely knew Seth, yet the minutes I spent in his company were so loaded with chemistry there was no point denying the truth.

All other thoughts about Grams and Finn and secrets and demons, muddled and conflicted as they were by feelings of betrayal and anger, needed to wait for another day because I had only hours until I could be with Seth again.

I took off down the hall, beelining for my desk, a notepad, and a pen. This time, I wouldn't waste my precious minutes with Seth feeling overwhelmed or confused.

This time, I'd be ready.

Dreamer's Log: Edith (daughter of Cecilia)
Day Twelve of March, Year 1753

Grandmother Agnes died today. She took with her the hiding place of the magic, and I know not where it is.

CHAPTER TEN

I wrote a list.

For all my confidence that *this* time I'd be prepared, I knew all too well the sensations of being overcome by Seth's *charms*, as the book described them. It was hard enough to think clearly when I was with him during the day and he was supposed to be at his weakest, but he'd demonstrated the potential nighttime strength of his power when he'd compelled me to leave him after the attack. As he'd ordered me away, he'd continued to attract me, and it had been desire that had given me the strength to be stubborn.

Having felt these effects firsthand, I could very well understand how a person would happily give up their blood to a vampire. I'd have allowed my assailant to bite my neck had Seth not been there to rescue me. I'd have begged to feel the strange vampire's cold lips on my skin, pleaded for him to drink my blood. I trembled at the memory.

So, I wrote a list.

I ended up with a page of questions I could ask Seth to keep our conversation on track. It included trivial things, like his favorite books and music, among more difficult subjects, including the reasons why he didn't kill his prey. The how of that question intrigued me more than it horrified me, and I spent some time wondering about the practicalities of giving a vampire only some of my blood.

I fooled myself into thinking my conversation with Seth would be easy.

I kept to myself for the rest of the afternoon. I showered, and then dressed in denim shorts and a vintage tee. I'd washed my hair, so I devoted twenty minutes to weaving it into a braid instead of twisting into my usual messy topknot.

Finn sent me another text, and I replied in as few characters as I could without making him suspicious. He accepted my claim that my headache had worn me out and I'd be lying low that night, but he promised to visit me in the morning with a latte from my favorite coffee shop. I decided to worry about that later, along with all the other concerns I was resolutely shelving for the time being.

When Grams returned from her excursion, she came straight to my room to check on my health. I was sitting at my desk by then, and I assured her I felt much better but gave her the excuse of homework and a deadline as the reason why I wouldn't join her for dinner. I had no appetite anyway, but I couldn't stomach the idea of making small talk with Grams while this enormous secret sat between us. I would need to find a way around my anxiety eventually but, for now, avoidance seemed as good a tactic as any.

The minutes ticked by at an interminable pace, and I ran out of distractions. I resorted to games of sudoku on my smartphone, but it was hard to lose myself in the challenging math puzzles. My eyes kept returning to the clock.

At about nine-thirty p.m., Grams again returned to my room, this time to wish me safe dreams and a good night. She did feel my forehead again for fever but must have been satisfied with the temperature of my skin because she made no comment on it. Instead, she fished around in the pocket of her dressing gown and pulled out a small white organza pouch. She offered it to me, and I took it.

Inside was a fine silver necklace, with a silver charm attached. I turned it over in my fingers. It was a sharp, slim dagger as long as my shortest finger, the hilt connected to the chain by a small link so, when worn, the blade would point downward.

It was beautiful. It was disturbingly ironic.

"I think it's time you had this. I was going to wait until your birthday but"—she paused, and her brow furrowed very slightly—"something tells me I shouldn't wait."

"This is so silly," I protested but it sounded hollow. I didn't feel frustrated or irritated by Grams's superstitions anymore—I couldn't, now I knew them all to be true—but I'd made a promise to Seth to keep up the pretense. I'd do my best, but duplicity wasn't my strong suit.

My words seemed to confirm something for Grams because she sighed resignedly. I met her eyes but held my tongue, too scared I might say the wrong thing. She nodded so imperceptibly it may have been my imagination, and then stepped around me to fasten the chain about my neck.

The dagger was cool and heavy against my skin. It would take time for me to forget it was there. I raised my hand to where it sat on my chest and was surprised by how much comfort I felt at its presence.

"You will tell me if you dream, won't you, Riley?"

Grams seemed older, smaller, and my heart broke a little. I could promise her this much with an honest oath.

"Yes, Grams, I will."

She nodded as though she believed me and left the room.

Grams suspected something. I had to believe it had to do with dreaming. I couldn't imagine any circumstances in which she'd willingly allow me to consort with vampires, even good ones with whom she was on amicable terms. That thought gave me another item to add to my list of questions for Seth. How did he and his family know my great-grandmother, and what did they want from her? I'd always known Grams felt the need to protect me from demons, but I never anticipated I'd feel such a powerful urge to do the same for her.

I absentmindedly played with the dagger as I reviewed and rewrote my questions, and the silver became warm in my fingers. I heard Grams stir at half-past eleven. She went to the kitchen to pour herself a glass of water, and I strained to listen as she returned to her bedroom and closed the door. I worried that she'd be sleeping too lightly when Seth arrived, and my impatience started to fray into panic. I paced back and forth in my small room, trying to expel the frenetic energy.

At fifteen minutes after midnight, I put my ear to Grams's door. Her snoring was barely audible, but clear enough that I believed her to be asleep. The sensation of nervous anticipation only heightened as I stepped lightly down the stairs and opened the front door.

My body softened, every muscle turning to water, as I looked at Seth standing inhumanly still on my porch. His mouth was quirked in the way that made my stomach flutter, and I wondered if he'd grown more beautiful since the night before.

I took an involuntary step forward. He took an immediate step back. A shadow passed over his face as his eyes flickered over my neck, and I touched the silver dagger, hanging flagrantly on its silver chain. I opened my mouth to explain it was new, but in an instant his face returned to its usual expression—confident and amused.

"Hello," he said with a smooth bow. "Here I am, as requested."

I gripped the piece of paper in my pocket, with my questions scrawled across one side, and recalled myself enough to shake off some of my stupor.

"Let's go around back," I said softly, stepping outside and closing the door behind me. "I'm not entirely sure Grams is sound asleep."

"She is," Seth replied. "I wouldn't be here otherwise."

"How do you know that she's sleeping?"

He raised an eyebrow and smiled secretively. "I have many talents," he replied unhelpfully.

I made a mental note to add a question about those *many talents* to my list.

I headed for the rear of the house, stepping lightly on the timber decking of the veranda. It wrapped around the house entirely, and it was one of the few things I loved about the place. I settled myself in one of the two cozy outdoor chairs Grams and I used for reading. We'd put layered rugs underneath them and a little side table between. Faded scatter cushions, on the seats and over the floor, rounded out the nook. None of our furniture was new or fashionable, but I liked the shabby, bohemian aesthetic.

Seth sat in the chair opposite me. He didn't sink into it the way I did. His back remained straight, his body on the edge of the seat as though he was prepared to spring up again at any moment. I readjusted my posture, so I didn't feel like such a sloth.

I opened my mouth to speak but my voice cracked. Ignoring the heat of embarrassment that crept up my neck, I cleared my throat and began again. "I have some questions."

"I thought you might."

I put my hand in my pocket again, and my fingers brushed the paper hidden there. I felt ridiculous at the idea of reading from it while he watched, but I also didn't think I could manage to stay on topic without a script. Desperation to understand him won out over self-consciousness, so I extracted the crumpled list, smoothed it out in my lap, and prepared to begin the interrogation.

Dreamer's Log: Edith (daughter of Cecilia)
Day Twenty-Eight of April, Year 1758

Yesterday, I birthed my daughter, and I did not die.

On the night she began to grow in my womb, I dreamed her arrival would break the curse that took my mother and grandmother. Yet only this morning, when I looked upon her and knew for certain she was real, did I accept that my reading of the dream was true. Never again will I doubt what I see when I sleep, or my interpretation of its meaning.

Now, I pray that I will live long enough to see my girl grow to be a woman.

I have named her Margaret in the hope that she will bring to our line the insight and understanding of our ultimate matriarch. The dream in which that wise old woman hid the magic may have been lost, but perhaps I can find another way forward.

Today, we begin again.

CHAPTER ELEVEN

Seth looked at the piece of paper in my hands warily, as if it were capable of jumping up and biting him.

"What is that?"

"It's a list," I said archly, refusing to be cowed into giving it up.

"A list?"

"Mm-hm." I made a show of reading it so I could avoid his eyes—the less he distracted me, the better—and cleared my throat. "Question one. What is your name and age?"

"That's two questions," he countered, and I sensed suppressed mirth in his tone.

"Does it matter?" I replied defensively.

He considered me, his face so still I could almost see his mind working. I prayed he'd go along with my little game. If he refused, I had no idea what to do next.

"Seth Callaghan. Eighteen."

"You can't really be eighteen," I argued, recalling the information in Grams's book.

Vampires were immortal, created hundreds of years ago

by a powerful demonic overlord. How was it that Seth looked to be my age, his brothers a handful of years more than that, and Perry was old enough to be his father? The numbers didn't add up.

"You are right," he agreed carefully. "I was eighteen when I was created and have been eighteen ever since."

"Created?"

"Yes, by the Master of Fear." He watched me. I waited. "In 1578."

I blinked in astonishment. "You're…more than four hundred and fifty years old?"

"I am."

Apparently, every answer Seth had for my prepared questions was going to trigger a round of newer, more urgent queries. It was too much of a struggle to keep up, so I returned to the page.

"Tell me about your family."

"That's not a question," he teased.

"Will you tell me about your family, please?"

"Perry is my father," he said. "Noel and Leo, my brothers. Felicity, my sister. Adeline and Van are not our family in the biological sense, but we adopted one another many, many years ago because we share certain philosophies on life." He smiled as though he'd made a joke.

"Your mother?" I asked quietly. I knew how sensitive a question this might be.

"Lost," he replied simply.

I shared the heartache of losing a mother and I didn't press him on it.

I moved onto silly things—books, music, hobbies—and he answered—modern literature, classical music, travel and art—with good humor and what appeared to be relief. When it felt as though I'd softened him a little, I hit him with the bigger questions.

"A vampire's existence is sustained by desire for blood and for pain," I declared and then shrugged uncomfortably. "I'm paraphrasing, but what I want to know is, why don't *you* desire blood or pain?"

"You've been reading up on me," he murmured, eyes narrowing.

I could sense he knew my questions were about to get more pointed, but I had no intention of backing down. I wondered if it was imagination that the short time so far with Seth seemed to have desensitized me to his power—though I still thought it best to not look at him directly.

"You're right, of course," he said. "Traditional vampires find their only pleasures in blood and pain, and I crave those things in much the same way. You need to know that, Riley. We all have impulses, some more powerful and more unsavory than others."

"I don't understand," I admitted.

He shook his head. "I'm not being clear, so your confusion is my fault." He looked up at the stars as he collected his thoughts, and then tried again. "Like all vampires, I feed on blood to exist, but after so many years, I need relatively little. I only ever take what I absolutely must, and that does not require me to drain a human of his lifeblood. Riley, I do not kill humans and neither does my family. In fact, we've become accustomed to surviving on animal blood. As for the pain…it's an optional extra, you might say. We do not need it to survive so I choose to abstain from that, among other things. I've discovered there are other ways to experience pleasure in this world."

His answer, again, created more questions than it answered.

"What do you do for pleasure?" I asked, stumbling over the last word. I prayed it was too dark for him to see the hot rush of blood creeping up my neck.

"It depends on my mood."

"Oh." I looked down at my notes but, more than anything written there, I was curious about something else he'd just said. "How do you drink blood without killing a person? I thought vampires took every drop."

"That is the conventional way, yes, but it's been almost five hundred years since we were created and much has changed."

"Will you tell me how it works?"

He hesitated, and I was certain he didn't want to share the specific details with me but then, inexplicably, he answered.

"If I were to drink the blood of a human, I would visit them at night and convince the donor I am a dream," he said slowly. I kept my expression carefully neutral. "I'd request a share of their blood and, if they agreed, I'd take it. They may wake feeling tired, with a small wound they cannot recall receiving, but the experience is not dangerous."

"So, all the stories about beautiful demons seducing humans at night are true?" I asked cheekily.

The crease between his brows softened and the concern in his eyes gave way to a mischievous sparkle. He smiled devilishly. "They are," he said.

"Not lies unfaithful men and women told their medieval priests to explain away infidelities?" I bantered, enjoying the change in his demeanor.

He laughed and I warmed at the sound. "I suppose one does not necessarily cancel out the other."

"Do many people deny you?"

"Some," he mused. "We have a theory that the old superstitions, though generally considered forgotten, still linger in the ancient memories of certain humans, and their instincts to refuse us are strong, especially in sleep. And a great many people wear silver these days, which tends to make hunting more difficult." His smile was self-mocking.

I nodded and opened my mouth to ask another question when he stiffened and scanned the darkness around the house as though searching for something. His eyes attached to some faraway, invisible target, but it was a few more moments before I could see anything of note.

Two people walked out of the shadows and into my yard, their pale faces incandescent by the half-moon in the sky.

Felicity and Van.

I looked to Seth, hoping his expression would tell me whether I should be afraid, but his face was very still.

I hadn't yet had a reason to speak to Felicity or Van. They kept to themselves at school, as did Seth—with everyone but me. Felicity shared the perfectly straight lines of Seth's face, rounded subtly into feminine loveliness. Her dark blonde hair was cut into a blunt bob, and she walked confidently although she was tiny. This close, I could see that Van's hair was a touch darker than Felicity's, warm ash, with a slight wave. He was just half a head taller than his girlfriend, and as solidly built as she was ethereal.

"Hello, Riley," Felicity said. Her voice had a sing-song quality to it that was very attractive, and I relaxed a little at the sound.

"What are you doing here, Liss?" Seth demanded. He didn't sound alarmed, only annoyed.

"Saving you from yourself," she replied, arching an eyebrow.

"I'm fine, but thank you for the concern."

Felicity sighed. "You may think you're fine, but this is not a good idea." Her eyes flickered to me.

"Has something happened?" he asked sharply.

"Nothing to worry about, but this is not helping."

I expected Seth to continue arguing but he only nodded and ran his fingers through his dark hair. He tousled it in a way that made it look more styled, not less.

"All right." He glanced at me, then returned to Felicity. "I'll follow you."

"Seth, no."

"I said, I'll follow you."

Van lightly touched Felicity's arm and her mouth flattened. "Fine," she huffed. "If you don't catch up in two minutes, I'll turn around and come right back."

Seth nodded. "I'll overtake you in one."

She rolled her eyes as though Seth were boasting, and then turned to me. "It's nice to meet you, Riley," she said.

Her face was open and friendly, and I smiled back at her reflexively. "It's nice to meet you, too."

"Two minutes," she warned Seth, and then she and Van sped from the porch, crossing my yard faster than was humanly possible. They shot into the shadows and disappeared.

Seth turned to me. "I have to cut our evening short."

I nodded reluctantly, aware there had been some subtext in his short exchange with his sister. I assumed it was vampire business. I doubted her concern was for my welfare.

He stood quietly for what seemed a painfully long time, no emotion that I could see written on his beautiful face. My heart fluttered fitfully as I stared into his eyes.

"Close your eyes," he directed, and I shut them instantly. "I enjoyed spending time with you tonight," he said. Slow, cold fingers swept the hair off my forehead, and my skin pebbled—I didn't think it was due to the chill of his skin this time. I sensed him move closer and I tilted my head a little, wondering if he were going to kiss me—hoping he would kiss me. The smell of him was intoxicating. I could hear him murmuring, but I couldn't make out the words.

The world no longer felt real, and the humming in my blood reached an almost painful crescendo. Strong, cold arms slid around my body, and I distantly registered the sensation of being lifted before I tumbled into sleep.

Dreamer's Log: Edith (daughter of Cecilia)
Day Fifteen of July, Year 1774

My Margaret is one to be reckoned with!

It is not often we cross the succubus. The female dream demon, perhaps, has more sense than her male counterpart, or more likely finds mortal men easier prey. Nevertheless, our line has faced some few over the years, those who thought they might be the one powerful enough to seduce us, steal our souls, and suck our blood. This most recent example was like all others, arrogant to the point of stupid.

It was painfully difficult to let Margaret take the lead—to me, she will always be but a babe in swaddling clothes—but it was to Margaret the succubus came, and to Margaret the duty fell. And there comes a time in all our lives when we must let our daughters test their strength: of spirit and of blood and of magic. I can only be grateful I was alive to observe—and be ready to intervene should she need assistance.

But of course, she did not! Oh, what a spectacle she was! That foul succubus stole into my daughter's mind and—poof! The demon was dead in an instant.

CHAPTER TWELVE

When I opened my eyes again, the morning sun lit my room, and I was sprawled out under my bed covers.

I'd slept soundly the rest of the night.

I strained to remember what had happened. I couldn't recall what Seth and I had talked about after Felicity and Van had been and gone, but I did remember what Seth had told me earlier about his hunting strategies.

I couldn't help myself. I checked my body all over for a wound, a puncture, anything that would indicate Seth had managed to persuade me to give him my blood. I found nothing and then felt silly. I hadn't dreamed, of course—I had no memory of being visited in the night by a beautiful, enchanting stranger—so obviously I had no unexplained injuries.

I fell back onto the mattress and startled myself by laughing. I should have been afraid but all I could focus on was Seth, and I could never be afraid of him. I quietly thanked Grams for telling me all her stories over the years. Somehow, she had prepared me for this moment even though

I'd fought her every step of the way. My anger had mellowed, I realized, and I looked forward to the moment we could be honest about everything. She'd be thrilled to have me on her side, finally. I pushed away a surge of guilt about all our previous disagreements and promised myself I'd find a way to make it up to her.

My phone chimed and I picked it up from my bedside table.

Finn.

He was on his way over with the latte he'd promised, and his text was a friendly warning to expect him at the front door in ten minutes.

Normally, I'd rush to brush my teeth and change into something more presentable than my pajamas but I was still in my shorts and tee from last night and, apparently, my rage at Finn hadn't softened the way it had for Grams. I didn't know how I was going to maintain my temper, so I spent those few minutes trying to cool my head.

Grams answered the knock at the door, and I heard her leave with Harry. He'd offered to take her shopping that morning, I suddenly remembered, and now I was panicked. Grams's company would have made confronting Finn impossible. Now, we'd be alone, and I had only my own self-control standing between my secret and my anger.

I wasn't sure which had the upper hand.

I left my room and made extra noise as I brushed my teeth and fixed my hair, so Finn would know I was awake.

I changed my clothes, then made my bed and straightened the papers on my desk. When I couldn't delay any longer, I stomped inelegantly down the stairs.

Finn waited in the living room, sitting on the edge of the sofa with two takeaway coffee cups balancing in a cardboard tray. There was a paper bag wedged between them, and I was sure my favorite pastries were inside.

"You look like you're feeling better," he said, standing and handing me a cup and the paper bag. The look on his face was relieved, as though he really had been worried about me.

"I do feel better," I agreed shortly.

I took my breakfast and headed into the kitchen. In the rush of all that had happened since Lizzie's party, I'd conveniently forgotten how much I loved Finn. It was more than a crush, but it also didn't feel like the urgent, chemical attraction I had for Seth. I most definitely didn't think of Finn as a brother but, like a brother, there was nobody in the world who knew me as well as Finn. I could rely on him for anything and talk to him about everything.

With certain foreboding, I knew things weren't going to end well today. My emotional strength was spent.

He followed me to the kitchen and joined me at the small table. I ate while he talked about Lizzie's party. I nodded and murmured in all the right places, but I had no enthusiasm for the conversation.

"Okay, what's up?" he demanded, putting down his coffee. "Are you still angry at me about the party?"

I scrambled to remember what he was talking about, and I thought about how he'd made me feel foolish for believing he might be interested in me romantically. It seemed so ridiculous now, and irrelevant.

"No," I answered.

"You're not yourself, Rae. What's going on?"

I picked apart my pastry, avoiding his eyes and berating myself for not putting on a better act. I wondered if I had meant it when I told Seth I could go about my life as though nothing had changed, pretending that I didn't know he was a vampire and that Finn had kept this enormous secret from me for the entire duration of our five-year friendship. I had meant it in the moment but, deep down, I'd always known it was an impossible promise.

I didn't answer Finn's question, but I met his eyes. I glared at him, willing him to confess to me what I already knew to be true. It occurred to me that I didn't have to admit I knew his secret if he told me about it first. I'd found the loophole I needed.

I didn't have to wait long.

We stared at each other in a stalemate that lasted no longer than thirty seconds. I could see the confusion playing out across his face. Worry, uncertainty. Disbelief, denial. We knew each other better than the dialogue in our favorite movies, and I suspected that for every expression I read on his face, my own mirrored it in subtle ways that Finn could read as easily.

A whole conversation passed between us without a spoken word. I wouldn't be the first to talk. He owed me that.

"Rae," he began, and then stalled.

"Yes?"

"What do you know?"

"What do you *think* I know?"

"Come on. What's this about?"

"You *know* what this is about."

He ran his fingers through his hair, the way he always did when trying to straighten out his thoughts, but this time I was reminded of Seth doing the same last night when confronted by his sister. I didn't like how uncomfortable I felt comparing the two of them, even unintentionally.

"Rae, I can't…." He shifted in his seat. "I need you to tell me first. Please?"

I held my stare, debating my next move.

"Vampires," I whispered, analyzing his face.

He said nothing, but his shoulders dropped. He lowered his face into his hands, elbows on the table, and rested there for the longest moment. I watched, refusing to feel sorry for him. Now wasn't the time to get soft.

"I can't believe you didn't tell me."

"I couldn't," he whispered, his face hidden in his hands.

"You could have," I argued. "You *should* have."

He shook his head. I saw no reason for him to not be honest now—I already knew the truth. His reluctance to be open with me spurred my temper.

When he finally raised his eyes, I was surprised to see anger mirrored there. What reason did *he* have to be mad at *me*? He had this all backward.

"Who told you?" he ground out between clenched teeth.

"What does it matter?"

"It matters. Was it Grams?"

I stared him down, refusing to confirm one way or another. I didn't really believe I could keep my promise to Seth now, but I was determined to go down fighting.

"It was *him*, wasn't it?"

I didn't reply but, again, Finn picked up on something in my face because he roughly pushed back his chair and stood, fists clenched at his sides.

"This is unbelievable!" His voice was raised, his face dark.

"At least one person in my life was honest with me!" I yelled back.

"That's a low thing to say. Grams has told you the truth from the beginning. It's your own fault you've always refused to believe her!"

And then I was on my feet, too, the blood thumping in my ears. "So, you admit you've lied to me for five years? Some best friend you are."

Again, he ran his hands through his blonde waves. He was struggling to say the right things and I fought against the instinct to sympathize.

"I *couldn't* tell you the whole truth," he said, sounding almost defensive. "I made a promise to Grams, and I meant it. She wanted to be the one to tell you."

"Our whole friendship has been based on lies! I can't believe anything you say to me, now or ever again."

His voice returned to its usual volume. "Come on, Rae. That's not fair. I never wanted to keep things from you."

"I have no way of knowing if that is true," I retorted.

"Riley, I'm sorry. You can't know how many times I've wanted to tell you everything. I wish…I wish I had been the one to tell you. Hell, I wish I had no idea about any of it myself! Life would be better if we were both completely clueless."

He walked into the living room, leaving me standing alone in the kitchen. The adrenaline of our argument had faded, and my impulse now was to repair the damage.

My emotions were seriously short-circuited.

I followed Finn to the other room and sat across from him on the wide sofa. I said nothing, unsure how to pick up the conversation.

"I can't believe he told you," he whispered, his voice loaded with incredulity.

"He didn't," I admitted. "Not exactly."

Finn looked at me skeptically.

"Seriously. I…was attacked, the night of the party."

The color drained from Finn's face. "Attacked? How?"

"Vampire," I replied, my voice strained. I hadn't dwelled on the terror of that night and reliving it now wasn't pleasant.

"Rae, what happened?"

"I left Lizzie's party, planning to walk home, and there was a man—I thought it was a man—standing in the road. He called to me and touched my face. He was strange but I didn't understand why at the time. Then Seth…." I trailed off as Finn's expression shifted from horror to anger. "He saved me, Finn. He came out of nowhere and saved me. That's why I was so jittery when I saw you in the driveway. It had only just happened."

Finn shook his head. "This is all my fault."

"How do you figure that?"

"I never should have left your side at the party. I should have driven you home and made sure you were safe."

"Finn, this isn't your fault. There's nothing you could have done."

He shook his head again, this time disagreeing with me. "What happened to the vampire who attacked you?"

"Seth took care of it."

His eyes narrowed and his head cocked to the side as he contemplated his next words. "You do understand that Seth is a vampire too?"

"I do," I confirmed.

"And that doesn't bother you?"

"He's not like the others, and don't try to argue with me. I know it's true, and so do you, otherwise there's no way Grams would have had his father in our house."

Finn sighed. "What a mess. So, I guess you've told Grams? It's all out in the open now." He sounded hopeful.

"Not exactly," I said sheepishly.

"Rae, what have you done?"

"Seth seems to think he'll be in serious trouble if his family finds out he's exposed them. Apparently, you've all been sworn to keep this secret from me—and for some reason I don't understand, you're all tripping over yourselves to do as Grams tells you to do. So, I promised Seth I wouldn't tell anyone I know the truth." I looked at him meaningfully. "You and I were never supposed to have this conversation."

He smiled crookedly. "You couldn't help yourself, could you?"

"Finn, you're my best friend. I can't pretend. Not with you."

"What a mess," he repeated. "So, where does this leave us?"

"I need to ask you a favor," I replied.

He looked at me warily. "What favor?"

"I need you to keep Seth's secret. Nobody can find out he's let the cat out of the bag. That means Grams and Harry and Perry can't be told that I know the truth."

"Rae, come on. That's a big ask—all for a vampire who, by the way, may not be your usual mail-order bloodsucker, but is still on my watch list. I don't like the guy, or his family. It's not my problem that he screwed up."

"*I* care, Finn. Please, for me?" When he faltered, I pressed my advantage. "You owe me this."

I watched his face until he met my eyes, and then I contemplated putting on my pathetic "please" expression but decided it wasn't the right time.

"How long is this going to last?" Finn asked, sounding defeated.

"Just until my birthday," I answered in a rush. "Seth seems to think that's when Grams is planning to tell me everything anyway."

Finn nodded unhappily. "Fine. I'll keep his secret—but only because he saved you on Friday night, and only because you asked me to. This isn't for his benefit, do you understand?"

"Yes, Finn. Thank you."

He shrugged. "Whatever."

"Did you still want to hang out today?" I asked. I hadn't thought beyond this conversation, and my stomach twisted at the idea that Finn might pull away from me now that I'd put Seth between us.

"Why do you ask? Have you had a better offer?"

I could tell he was doing his best to sound like his usual flippant self, but his voice was a little sharp.

"Nope," I assured him, trying to sound casual but hoping he'd pick up the import of my answer. "You're it."

He smiled a little. "I guess I can stay for a while," he said. "What did you have in mind?"

Dreamer's Log: Edith (daughter of Cecilia)
Day Fifteen of June, Year 1785

Finally! I may have found a way forward—not the path I sought, I grant you, but a possibility I cannot ignore. A flicker of hope where there has been none thus far, and how can I be expected to turn my back on it?

Last night a soul screamed in the aether. Of course, this is not uncommon—too many aimless spirits are tormented by those creatures of the devil that live trapped in the spaces between life and death—but this scream was unlike any I've heard before. It was the wail of an incubus whose heart had been broken.

I know it sounds a fancy, but I also know it to be true.

I stood in the dream a long time, listening to him shriek his pain, and when it ended I was left with the overwhelming certainty that our future will look different to that which we have always envisioned, and the past we have sought to recapture.

Without the magic in our safekeeping, we are vulnerable, here on Earth and in the dream. It is an uncomfortable yet unavoidable truth, and though it hurts me to admit it, we simply do not know how long this will go on. One day, we may be overcome. One day, our existing defenses may not be enough.

But I do declare that no more need it be a matter of us and them, because out there is an incubus seeking a salve for his sorrow. Out there is a dream demon who feels the type of torture normally reserved for those of us with human hearts.

Out there, somewhere, is a creature of darkness who would be our ally.

Together with Margaret, I will devise a plan to locate our heartsick incubus and ask him how we might go about constructing a mutually beneficial partnership. I fear I know how to find him, and though it will risk both Margaret's safety and mine, I find myself worrying more at how we might convince those brave mortal men who so devotedly guard us in our waking hours that an alliance with a demon has been deemed necessary by fate.

CHAPTER THIRTEEN

Finn met me at my house at eight a.m. on Monday morning. His recent habit of walking me to school had survived the weekend, and it gave me hope that things could be all right between us.

We'd spent Sunday afternoon doing the things we'd normally do together—we watched a movie, went for a hike, finished our math homework—but there was an uneasiness to our conversation that saddened me. I tried to convince myself it was all in my head, but deep down I knew that Finn could sense it, too. It was almost a relief when he'd gone home for the night.

The twelve-hour break seemed to have reset his mood. He arrived upbeat, his infectious grin in place, and I sagged in relief at the way he looked at me. It was the way he always looked at me.

Three minutes into our walk, he hit me with a comment I wasn't expecting.

"I thought you'd have a thousand questions about all this," he said. "Aren't you curious?"

I was such an idiot. It hadn't occurred to me that *Finn* might be able to resolve the unknowns I had scrawled on my list of things to ask Seth. I'd been so preoccupied about how this development would affect our relationship for the worst, I hadn't considered that Finn was still my best friend, only now, we had no secrets.

"I do! I have a million of them. Why? What do you know?"

He chuckled. "More than you do."

I rolled my eyes. "Do I have to drag it out of you?"

It felt good to spar with him, even if the subject was a little dicey.

"Maybe," he teased, but when I flicked a twig at him, he threw up his hands and laughed easily. "Okay, okay. Ask me anything. I'll do my best to answer to your satisfaction."

Mollified, I walked a little distance in silent thought, working out the best way to start. My questions for Finn weren't the same as those I wanted to ask Seth, though they weren't too far different. I said the first thing that came to mind.

"Why did you pretend all this time to agree with me?" I asked quietly. "We've always made fun of Grams and Harry. We swore we'd never be like them."

Saying the words out loud, I realized that learning the truth had left me feeling like a fool. Finn had let me believe we were in this together.

"Rae, I do agree with you," he said, and I appreciated him taking me seriously. "I have no desire to go into the family business."

"The family business?"

He kicked at the ground as he walked. Finn struggled with this, too, and I paid closer attention to his answer. There was more to this than his promise to Grams.

"Generation after generation of vampire legends, left to our families to remember and protect and pass down. The truth about demons—what an inheritance for the kids, eh?" He snorted. "I'd sooner have a regular life with regular problems."

"Have you seen a vampire before?"

"Perry and Harry have known each other forever. Perry was a friend of my grandpa, and his father before him." He looked at me sideways. "You know that vampires are immortal, right? Perry's almost five hundred years old."

"Yeah," I said, trying not to appear surprised at his casual tone. He spoke of vampires as though they were everyday occurrences. I supposed, to Finn, they were.

"So, all that stuff about starting fresh, leaving behind our weird families, I meant every word of it."

"If your family has known…Perry's family for all this time, why do you hate them so much?" I'd been about to say "Seth's family," but thought better of it at the last minute. Finn didn't seem to pick up on my stumble. "Aren't you sort of friends?"

He snorted again. "I wouldn't say friends. It's more like uneasy allies."

"Allies?"

"They're the good guys, right?" His voice was thick with sarcasm. "We stay in touch to keep on top of what's new in the world of demons. If there are bad guys around, they give us a heads up."

"Are there usually…bad guys around?"

Finn was oblivious to the fact this information might trouble me. I only got the feeling that he was relieved—possibly even excited—that he didn't have to watch what he said around me anymore.

"Nope," he said, launching himself over a small boulder and landing lightly on his feet. "The only leech I'd ever met before is Perry. The rest of the family is new to me." He didn't mention Seth by name, and I wondered if the omission was deliberate. He didn't call out Felicity, or Adeline and Van, either. "They still make my skin crawl, no matter that they're supposed to be on our side."

"There *was* a bad guy here, over the weekend," I murmured. "The vampire who attacked me after Lizzie's party."

His steps faltered, and then stalled. Finally, he noticed that I couldn't be as blasé about this as he was.

"It won't happen again."

"How can you be so sure?"

He couldn't answer me, and we started walking again.

"Has Perry's family always lived nearby?" I asked.

Finn shook his head. "No. Vampires never stop in one place for very long, but then Perry arrived earlier in the summer and announced he had a house in the hinterlands."

"Oh." I wondered why they'd decided to stay and hoped they wouldn't leave again anytime soon.

Finn answered my unspoken thoughts. "I can't imagine they'll stick around long. This place doesn't suit them, with all the sunshine. It makes them too vulnerable. Our lives will go back to normal in no time."

"Right," I said.

We walked on and I asked no more questions because I didn't want any more answers.

Seth was waiting for me at the door to our history classroom. He leaned too casually against the doorjamb—the posture looked unnatural on him—but when he saw me approaching, he stood straight and smiled. I walked faster, my blood pulsing quicker, to get to him that much sooner.

"Hello," he said. "Did you have a good weekend?"

"You left without saying goodbye," I accused, taking myself by surprise. That wasn't what I had planned to say.

"I apologize," he said, an eyebrow raised. "I anticipated our farewell might have been a little drawn out had we done it the human way."

"The human way?" I flushed self-consciously as I wondered if he could mean what I hoped he did.

His answering smile was small and secretive. "Did you sleep well?" he asked, following me into the classroom.

"I did, actually."

"And the remainder of your weekend was pleasant?"

I busied myself at my desk, fussing with my textbooks and settling into my chair. Seth watched me with curiosity.

"Riley, is something wrong?"

I took a deep breath, inhaling his scent and taking advantage of its relaxing effects. "Finn knows."

Seth froze. I loudly cleared my throat and pretended to read while the room began to fill with students.

"I didn't mean for him to find out, but don't worry, he won't say anything," I murmured.

When he didn't reply, I looked up and found him staring down at me, his forehead creased, and the corners of his mouth turned down. "I do worry."

"You can trust Finn," I assured him.

He sighed and shook his head. "I'd like to believe that."

"Trust *me*," I pleaded.

"All right, everyone. Settle down."

Mr. Gersen started the class before Seth could say any more. Ten minutes later, after the teacher had set the tasks for the lesson, Seth slid a tiny piece of folded paper across the desk. I knew what was inside, so I began to prepare the words I'd need to convince Seth that Finn was on our side.

I hid the paper in my lap and opened it, taking care not to attract the teacher's attention, and gasped.

Seth had drawn a small sketch of a girl. She was almost in profile, her eyes cast down and her head tilted just enough to give the impression she was reading. She had a slender hand cupped around her neck. Her lashes were long, her lips full. Her hair was a messy knot tied at the top of her head, her choppy fringe catching on her lashes. On the near side, her exposed ear was decorated with six earrings of different shapes and sizes. The picture had been drawn in meticulous detail, with lines and shading in contrasting grays to indicate shadows and depth. Somehow, there was a flush to her cheeks, even though there was no color.

I couldn't quite believe that the picture was meant to be me, as I was at that very minute.

Seth watched my reaction with an unreadable expression. I swallowed self-consciously.

"You're very talented."

"I draw what I see," he replied.

I tried not to think too much about the picture for the remainder of the class. I tucked it away, first inside the cover of my textbook, then in my pencil case, then in the pocket of my schoolbag. Nowhere I put it seemed safe or sacred enough. As I retrieved it from its most recent hiding place, Seth smiled. He looked quite entertained.

"It's not funny," I mumbled.

"I didn't say it was," he replied, but he chuckled when he said it.

I blushed furiously and slipped the paper into the pocket of my shorts. That would have to do until I could hide it in a book at home.

Seth accompanied me to my next class, even though he should have headed to the other side of the campus, but I didn't object.

"Finn walks with you to school every day, and you walk home together," he said abruptly.

"Yes," I confirmed, wondering where he was headed.

"You spend the lunch hour with him, and most weekends."

"I do."

He nodded thoughtfully. "You have no classes together."

"No."

"And he attends sporting commitments four nights a week, plus Saturday mornings."

"Have you been spying on us?"

"Not exactly."

I waited for him to elaborate, and there was a lag in the conversation.

"Your nights are usually free, when you're home with your grandmother," he finally continued.

"They are."

He hesitated, and I wondered if I was imagining his discomfort. I couldn't think of anything that would shake Seth's cool demeanor, but he certainly seemed uneasy.

We arrived at my classroom, and I paused with him outside the door.

"Would you object to my visiting you occasionally, those times when you are free?" he asked.

"No, I wouldn't object," I said instantly.

"Riley, please understand what I am asking you. I'd like to visit you. Unsupervised. At night."

"I understand."

He grimaced. "I'm not sure you do. Perhaps you could think about it, at least for a day? I'll ask again tomorrow, when you've had an opportunity to consider my proposal with a cool head."

"My head is plenty cool. I don't need time to think about it," I replied stubbornly.

He smiled, and I sensed he'd shaken off whatever doubt had plagued him minutes earlier.

"I think I must insist." His cool hand brushed a strand of hair off my face, leaving the exquisite sting of static electricity on my skin, and then, too soon, he walked away.

"I can't believe you landed Seth Callaghan," a high, caustic voice said beside me.

It took a second to process the comment, and another to attach it to me.

"I haven't landed anyone, Lizzie," I said distractedly, too intent on watching Seth's retreat. Actually, I felt a little drunk. I wasn't convinced that daylight made all that much difference to the strength of his vampire ways. His effect on me was brutal, no matter the time of day.

"Get a clue, Riley," Lizzie snapped.

She walked away but left me with something to think about. Someone other than me thought Seth wanted to be more than friends, and I liked the way that felt.

Dreamer's Log: Margaret (daughter of Edith)
Day Two of December, Year 1799

We are close to six months shy of proclaiming it to be fifteen years since Mama had her dream about the ambivalent incubus, and thereby fifteen years that we have searched for him without luck.

To be fair, we have needed to move slowly, not having anticipated the extent of the unwanted effects of our hunting methods.

It has always been that in the dream we feel the press of demonic eyes on us, the breath on our skin, the touch on our souls. It is a discomfort we tolerate and, perhaps to some degree, we have become a little desensitized to it—or at least, we have learned to ignore it as best we can while we go about our work.

And yet now, there can be no doubt, following so many years of proof, that by standing in the dream and discarding all our usual safeguards—by letting our power ring out in the way of the siren in sailors' lore—that our magic calls not only to the mysterious incubus we seek, but to any dream demon inside the aether who happens to stray too close to our magic. The fire of our magic lures them out, as dear Agnes did once rightly claim—as the bright flame beckons the moth.

Never have the women of our line murdered so many incubi and succubi as Mama and I have in the last one-and-a-half decades.

I do confess, however, that as carefully as Mama and I searched when we were together, I have moved at an even slower pace since her death three years gone. I have found solitary dream walking not much to my liking, and so it is with great force of will that I commit myself to sending out my siren's call just three times in a year. On all but two occasions, I have been attacked. Of course, I was the victor in every instance, but I have never felt easy about such conflict. I seem not to have my mother's spark and strength.

This is all set to change almost immediately, as Johnna is almost eighteen and therefore we can expect her own power to shortly reach its majority. Perhaps then, with another witch at my side again, I will recover some of the courage I had when Mama was here to hold onto my hand, and we shall resume our schedule of twice-monthly summonses.

CHAPTER FOURTEEN

I walked to school the next morning determined to accept Seth's proposal. I refused to entertain any niggling doubts—about what Grams would say, about what Finn would think, about the undeniable fact that Seth was still a vampire—and focused instead on the night Seth saved me, the careful way he touched me, the portrait he sketched that was now pressed between the pages of my favorite book. Seth was a vampire, sure, but he wasn't *only* a vampire.

He was there at the door to our afternoon history lesson. His way of meeting me before our classes had quickly gained a sense of ritual, and it warmed me to see him standing there, tall and beautiful with his eyes on me.

"You look as though you need to tell me something," he observed.

"I do."

Seth had said he would ask again, so I waited.

He cocked an eyebrow, and then followed me into the classroom. When we'd taken our seats, he finally spoke.

"Riley, I've been reconsidering—"

I raised a hand to stop him.

"I've thought about it, like you asked, and I would still like to see you. At night. Alone. Just you and me."

His eyes crinkled a little at the corners as he grinned.

"I was contemplating retracting the offer. It occurred to me that most people would view our plan as reckless."

"Oh?" I said artlessly. "How so?"

He lowered his voice and leaned in conspiratorially. "Some people might say that a human who chooses to spend her time with a vampire has no regard for her own well-being."

"I suppose some people might say that," I said with excessive nonchalance, and used the excuse of opening my notebook and selecting a pen to avoid his gaze. I wasn't going to be talked out of this.

"Some people might say that it's inappropriate for teenagers to meet alone, at night, in secret."

I waved away his comment. "Old fuddy-duddies."

"Some people might say you've been bewitched by an immortal demon. They might wonder if you're thinking clearly. They might believe you've fallen under a spell, and your interest in the vampire boy is a product of magic, not…chemistry."

I did look at him then. A smile curved his lips, but it had a self-deprecating turn to it.

"Some people don't know what they're talking about," I said carefully. "I've had plenty of time to think about things, away from you and the influence of your *bewitchments*. I feel the same no matter where I am or who I'm with."

"And how do you feel, exactly?"

I froze. He very slightly moved closer, his eyes burning into mine. The words teetered on my lips, but I held a tight enough grip on sanity to know I would never confess how I felt before I knew for sure he felt the same way about me.

Mr. Gersen called the class to attention, and I was saved from having to answer Seth's question. He released my eyes, and his smile recovered some of its cocky confidence. I took an unsteady breath and opened my textbook.

Seth Callaghan was going to be the death of me.

In the end, Seth agreed to visit me that night. My afternoon, as a result, dragged on endlessly. My concentration was compromised, and I suspected my notes, which were woeful even under usual circumstances, would be particularly hard to decipher when I needed them again. I couldn't bring myself to care.

When school let out, I wasted no time locating Finn. He was waiting for me at our usual afternoon rendezvous point, but he wasn't alone.

"Hey, Lizzie," I interrupted, loudly and intentionally obnoxious.

She ignored me, her wide blue eyes glued to the object of her affection. "I'll see you tomorrow, Finn, and remember"

—Lizzie dropped her voice low with the pretense of sharing a secret, but her words were plenty loud enough for me to hear—"I'm always here if you need me."

She roughly brushed past me as she left, and I stumbled backward a little. She didn't apologize, and I didn't do her the favor of retaliating. I crossed my arms over my chest as I watched her walk away.

"What did she want?" I grumbled.

Finn didn't answer, and when I looked up at him, he was watching me with a smug grin.

"What?" I demanded roughly, and my cheeks burned with anger. I knew what he was getting at, and I wasn't *jealous* of Lizzie Porter.

He raised his arms in mock surrender and laughed. "I didn't say anything."

I rolled my eyes and started the walk home. Finn caught up to me within a few steps and easily matched my stride.

"What's the rush?" he asked.

"Nothing," I replied, reluctantly slowing my pace.

He grunted.

"Bad day?" I asked, not listening for his response. I'd already wiped worry about Lizzie and Finn from my mind. My thoughts had returned to Seth and our…date?

"Not yet," he said, sounding uncharacteristically serious.

That got my attention. "What's the matter?"

"The usual family stuff," he said with a shrug. "They've been worse since Perry's crew arrived."

"What do you mean, *worse*?"

Finn put an arm around my shoulders and pulled me in against his body. He was warm and familiar, and I didn't protest. "I guess I don't have to dance around the truth anymore."

"What a relief that must be. You've always had two left feet." He gave me a flat look, and I grimaced apologetically at my own sad joke. "Tell me everything."

"Harry has never given me too hard a time about hating all the vampire stuff," he said. His casual use of the word still startled me. "They've let me—and you—ignore it for the most part, but the last few weeks have been…different. They're putting the pressure on to take things more seriously."

"That makes no sense. The Callaghans are good—allies, right? There's nothing to be worried about."

"All vampires are killers, Rae. They're all addicted to blood. These ones are just in recovery."

I pondered that for a moment. It didn't resonate with my opinion of Seth, but something in Finn's voice worried me. I stepped out of the circle of his arm.

"Finn, what do your parents want you to do?"

He scrubbed at his face in frustration. "Monday meetings, to start with, and more *active participation* in our lifestyle. And that means getting more familiar with our friendly neighborhood vampires."

"That doesn't sound too bad," I said warily.

"Come on, Rae."

"Sorry," I muttered.

"Forget it," he said. "Let's talk about something else."

He didn't initiate a new conversation and neither did I, so we walked the rest of the way to my house in silence. I didn't feel the lack because the entire time I worried about what might happen if Finn was forced to spend more time with the Callaghans and, by extension, Seth.

"Dinner was lovely, thank you," Grams said, setting aside her cutlery.

I'd made grilled fish and a green salad, nothing fancy, but I'd volunteered to take care of dinner by myself as a way to keep my mind and hands occupied while I waited for the minutes to tick over. Now, I took our plates to the sink and began to wash the frying pan as I cataloged ways I could pass the time until Grams fell asleep. T-minus four hours. I had homework, but I doubted I had the capacity to concentrate. Perhaps I would listen to music or mindlessly scroll through videos on YouTube. That was always a dependable way to waste time.

"How was school today?" Grams asked.

"Fine," I replied absently.

"And Finn?"

"Also fine."

"How have Perry's children been settling in?"

I froze, and then quickly resumed scrubbing.

Grams hadn't mentioned Seth, Felicity, or Van since our conversation weeks ago, when she'd asked me to avoid them. I'd been thankful the subject hadn't come up. It made the task of hiding my admiration of Seth much more manageable.

I kept my back to her as I replied. "Fine, I think. They keep to themselves for the most part."

"I'm glad to hear that. It's for the best," she responded.

I murmured my agreement, and hastily wiped over the last of the dirty dishes. When they were done, I dried my hands and gave Grams a swift kiss on the cheek.

"Goodnight, Grams."

"Isn't it a little early to be going to bed?"

"I have a ton of homework," I lied. "I'm going to tuck up in bed with it. It's sure to put me to sleep early."

She nodded but her lips pursed. "All right," she said. "Good night, then. Safe dreams."

I bounded up the stairs two at a time, grabbed a set of clothes from my room, and locked myself in the bathroom. I showered and washed my hair—brushing and drying it properly would require another half an hour, and that seemed like a smart idea. I was getting more impatient by the minute.

The hours dragged. YouTube wasn't cutting it, so I picked up a copy of *The Lion, the Witch and the Wardrobe*—an old favorite that never failed to soothe me—but the words slid past my eyes without making an impression.

Eventually, Grams closed her bedroom door for the night. I had to force myself to stay put for another thirty minutes to ensure she was fast asleep before I started moving around the house.

As soon as the clock on my phone ticked over to ten-fifteen p.m., I crept down the stairs. Already, my body felt jittery, just knowing Seth was close.

I opened the front door, and he was there, waiting.

The relief of finding him on my porch, so still and so perfect, was a stark reminder that I still didn't entirely believe his interest in me was real. I'd subconsciously prepared myself for the possibility of being stood up, but I roughly sidelined that train of thought. I didn't want the distraction right now.

"I have a favor to ask you," he said, quickly and quietly.

"Another one?" I teased, stepping out onto the porch and closing the door behind me.

He smiled apologetically. "I have a little problem—two, actually. Felicity and Van. They're aware of our plan to spend time together and they're concerned. They've insisted on chaperoning."

"They're concerned for me?" It made no sense.

Seth shook his head slightly before stopping himself. "Not exactly," he admitted.

"They're concerned for *you*?" That made even less sense.

He laughed quietly. "In a manner of speaking. They worry about the nature of our relationship."

I blushed, and Seth closed his eyes for a moment before going on. "Aside from that, they do not think it's a good idea for us to meet out in the open in this way. I have to agree."

"Would you like to come inside?" I asked.

He hesitated. "No, thank you. There's a place not too far from here, where Felicity and Van and I go sometimes, to get away from things. Would you…would you come with us?"

My throat spasmed as I swallowed nervously. My mouth had gone dry and it hurt a little. "You want me to go with you, and Felicity and Van?"

He paced away, clenching and releasing his fists, and then turned back to me.

"Yes, I want that, but I also want you to refuse me. I cannot tell anymore which is safer for you."

"Safer for me?"

His comments were getting harder and harder to follow.

He grunted in frustration. "I only want you to be out of harm's way, Riley. I do not think there are other vampires out there tonight, so I do not believe you would be in immediate danger, even if I was to leave you alone, but I still would like to be near you so I know you are safe."

"The attack on Friday night was a case of wrong place, wrong time. What are the chances of being in that position again?" I tried to sound nonchalant but something in his tone had alarmed me.

He smiled crookedly. "You may be right," he agreed. "Perhaps I am too easily spooked." He brushed my cheek with his fingertips, pulling back quickly as though burned, and my body quivered involuntarily. "Will you come?"

"Seth." I jumped at the sound of Felicity's voice coming from nowhere and everywhere, and Seth dropped his hand. "Play fair," she admonished.

Seth's little sister stepped out from around the corner of the house, and Seth gave her a hard stare. "I'm trying," he said through gritted teeth.

She laughed a little, in that melodic way I'd noticed before, and then walked past Seth to me.

"Hello, Riley," she said. "Would you like to spend an hour or two with us—Seth, Van, me? You should know, this place we go to, this beach, cannot be reached by humans, so you'd have to trust us to get you there and get you home. It's unbelievably beautiful and I think you'd like it." She stepped closer then, between me and Seth, so that her lovely face obscured my view of him entirely. "You're free to say no." Her breath was gentle on my cheeks. It smelled sweet, like raspberries.

I shook my head, and she cocked hers as she tried to understand. I forced the words from my throat. "No, I don't want to say no. I want to go with you."

She smiled pleasantly. "Good to hear it."

Felicity moved out of my way and my eyes searched hungrily for Seth. He looked at me oddly, his mouth quirked a little differently, his brows drawn down a touch, and he held out his hand. "Shall we?"

My skin pebbled as my fingers met the cool, hard flesh of his hand. I couldn't speak, so I simply nodded.

Dreamer's Log: Johnna (daughter of Margaret)
Day Thirty-One of August, Year 1810

Mama has passed, and Sissy is but ten years old, so I face at best eight years of seeking our elusive demon with nothing but my own fortitude to keep me at the task. Sissy begs for the day she may stand strong by my side, but I fear I have inherited much of my mother's reticence toward walking the dream and facing down the monsters of hell. But I will go on. I am proud to admit that I have also inherited her sense of duty.

I often wonder if the erosion of my confidence can be laid, in part, at the feet of the vampires who seek to strike our mortal flesh. It is truly terrifying. Though we take great care to hide ourselves in the waking world, I can only conclude that our increased activity in the dream somehow also functions as a beacon to those who stalk their prey here on Earth. And to these vampires, I have no recourse. Our continued well-being is entirely dependent on understanding that which our dreams foretell, and how expeditiously our bodyguards can respond.

CHAPTER FIFTEEN

We walked around the back of the house, across the wide lawn, and into the bushland that surrounded us, moving deep into the shadows. I moved closer to Seth, not wanting to make a big deal of the fact I was terrified a spider, or its web, might attach itself to my face as I stumbled along, blinded by the darkness. He pulled me against his side protectively, and I shivered at the coolness of his body, but I didn't move away.

"We won't stay in the trees much longer," he murmured. "We'd like to get a little distance between us and the neighbors before we make a run for it."

"We're running there?"

That would be a problem. I wasn't wearing the right shoes.

Seth chuckled. "*We* are. You aren't."

I examined that from every angle. "I don't understand," I admitted, and he laughed again.

Van led our odd party as we wound our way through the darkness just inside the tree line. I glanced behind to see Felicity bringing up the rear, then redirected my eyes forward before I tripped and landed on my face. I tried to give Seth space to walk without me stepping on his toes, but he didn't seem encumbered by me. If anything, he held my hand a little tighter when I pulled away, and tucked me closer against his body. He didn't misstep once.

This part of bushland bordered the backyards of my neighbors. It took fifteen minutes of hiking before we were beyond the houses and into denser forest. It was another ten minutes before Van stopped for no reason I could work out. He stood eerily still and stared out at nothing, as though listening for something. I strained my ears but could hear only the sounds of insects and small, invisible animals moving through the underbrush. I stopped listening when my imagination threatened to send me into panic. I waited, uncertain what it was that I waited for.

"I think we can start," Van said at last. It was the first time I'd heard his voice, and, like the others, it was soothing and smooth, and very deep.

"Are you ready?" Seth asked. His eyes were excited, his face bright in the moonlight, and his goofy grin made him handsomely boyish. My breath caught and I nodded, wide-eyed. "May I?" He extended his arms, and I nodded again.

He lifted me quickly and easily, and cradled me against his chest as though I were a child. It was an odd sensation. It had been too long since I'd been small enough to be held like that.

"Close your eyes," he whispered. His cold breath tickled my skin, and I pressed my eyelids shut. His arms gently held me tighter, and I leaned my head against his chest, only a threadbare linen shirt between his skin and mine.

Seth flinched, hissing softly, and I looked up in surprise. His lips twisted in self-mocking, but his eyes were pinched with pain.

"Your earring," he murmured.

I yanked my hair out of its band, shook it out and rearranged it over my shoulder so it covered the silver in my right earlobe. I gently returned my head to its cold pillow, trying an angle that kept my ear off his skin. "Is that better?"

"Much," he said.

Then, he ran.

I wasn't jostled, I wasn't uncomfortable and, had I not already been told that he intended to sprint with me in his arms, I might have assumed he was standing still the entire time—albeit against a breeze that bordered on a gale. The wind whipped past, my cheeks burned, and my body tensed. Seth's arms tightened protectively in response.

We ran for so long that my muscles started to cramp, but I couldn't bring myself to relax or open my eyes. I was torn between terror and exhilaration, and eventually decided it was better to worry less about how I was feeling and focus more on the moment.

So, I concentrated on the feel of Seth's arms around my body. They were strong yet gentle, and cold through his shirt sleeves. I pressed my face against his chest. It was still and cool, with the hardness of lean, strong muscles made from stone.

It didn't heave with breathing, and I couldn't hear a beating heart. I breathed in deeply, letting the fresh scent of him soothe my nerves. Seth's thumb brushed my arm back and forth, and I couldn't control the goosebumps that sprang up at his wintry touch.

It was about twenty minutes before Seth came to a stop. The force of the wind stopped suddenly, and then his lips were at my ear. "We're here," he whispered.

I opened my eyes, and Seth carefully set me on the ground. He kept a light hand on my back as I regained my balance, only removing it when he was confident I wasn't going to pass out from the rush of being upright again. I grimaced in disappointment when he dropped his hand, but he didn't step away. He watched me expectantly, his expression as boyish and excited as it had been before we began our journey, and I admired his face with open-mouthed wonder.

His lips quirked as though he could read my mind, and then he placed his hands on my shoulders and turned me gently to face away from him. My resistance to being denied his beauty faded away at the sight before me.

It was a beach unlike any I'd seen before, and I'd lived on the coast for five years. Finn and I had explored north and south as far as the buses and trains would take us, searching out secret bays and quiet coves where I could paddle and read on the sand, and swells and reefs for him to surf and swim and snorkel. This…this place was something else entirely. It was unearthly, the way Seth was unearthly, and my response was to feel small and insignificant. I took a step forward, and another, my eyes drawn up, and up, and up.

The powder-soft sand was white, but that wasn't unusual. The beaches in this part of the world were always bright and clean. The sand was warm from the day's heat, and walking on it felt safe and familiar. Though I didn't give it much thought, I appreciated this sensation of home even as I marveled at all that was different.

Around me and overhead, a giant stone cave yawned against the horizon to the east and the sky above. It was built of rough streaky rock in shades of gold and bronze, washed out to grays in the moonlight, and slashed from this side to that with white lines that glowed fantastically. Through the tall, wide opening ahead of me and a little way in the distance, I could see gently heaving black water lapping against the shore, glinting at its tips with the light of the moon and quietly roaring with the song of the ocean. Above me, the stone cave opened to a circle of midnight air and a million stars. I stared up into the magic.

A cold, hard hand slipped into mine. "Incredible, isn't it?"

I nodded. *Incredible* didn't do it justice but I wasn't clever enough to improve upon it.

"Where are we?"

"Not too far along the coast, about fifty-odd kilometers south, but this stretch of beach is completely secluded. No human ever comes here. It's impossible to get to by land or sea. Van discovered it, and we come here most nights."

I looked around for Felicity and her quiet boyfriend, but they'd already left the cave and started up the beach. I barely made out their shadowy forms before they disappeared into the darkness.

"You only come here at night?" I asked, starting toward the mouth of the cave. I wondered what the beach looked like outside these rocky walls.

"It's restorative to be under the moon this way. We spend so much time in the sunlight here, and there's hardly any cloud cover to give us respite. It feels good to bathe in moonlight, without anything between us and the sky."

"You hate being in a place where the sun shines every day. Your clothes aren't suited to the heat and yet you insist on wearing them. You don't need to be in school, so I don't understand. Why are you here?"

I didn't know why I let curiosity get the better of me. I was stupid to bring this up, in case the idea hadn't occurred to him yet, but I wanted to know.

"Perry wants us here, for now," Seth said.

It had the feel of being only half an answer, but I jumped on it with relief.

"Grams insists we live here, too, even though she doesn't like the heat," I replied, empathizing with the parental-control factor. "I've tried to persuade her that somewhere cooler would suit her better, but she's stubborn about it. I don't like the sun very much either. I burn too easily."

Seth laughed. "Me, too."

"The sun doesn't really burn you, does it?" I asked, surprised. I scanned his porcelain face for evidence of sun damage.

"Not exactly, but we are weakest in sunlight. Our strength and speed are compromised during the day, particularly under a clear sky and when the sun is at its zenith. That also somewhat explains the long clothes." He plucked at the sleeve of his shirt irritably. "Our skin draws attention, so it's prudent to keep it covered but, more importantly, the more exposed it is to the light, the more vulnerable we become. It's an uncomfortable feeling."

My memory skipped back to the information I'd read in Grams's book, and the line about defeating a vampire came floating to the surface.

"Does the sun weaken you so much that you could be overcome by a human?" I asked.

"A human?" Seth echoed, his brows furrowing. "No."

"Oh." I stared out over the ocean and wondered how reliable Grams's book could possibly be if it was wrong on that fairly important point, even if it had been correct about the silver.